THE OLD DIE YOUNG

MYSTERIES BY RICHARD LOCKRIDGE

The Old Die Young
The Tenth Life
A Streak of Light
Dead Run
Or Was He Pushed?
Death on the Hour
Not I, Said the Sparrow
Write Murder Down
Something Up a Sleeve
Death in a Sunny Place
Inspector's Holiday

Preach No More
Twice Retired
Troubled Journey
A Risky Way to Kill
Die Laughing
A Plate of Red Herrings
Murder in False-Face
With Option to Die
Murder for Art's Sake
Squire of Death
Murder Can't Wait

Murder Roundabout

OTHER BOOKS BY RICHARD LOCKRIDGE

One Lady, Two Cats
A Matter of Taste

The Empty Day
Encounter in Key West

Mr. and Mrs. North

BOOKS BY FRANCES AND RICHARD LOCKRIDGE
MR. AND MRS. NORTH

Murder by the Book
Murder Has Its Points
The Judge Is Reversed
Murder Is Suggested
The Long Skeleton
Voyage into Violence
Death of an Angel
A Key to Death
Death Has a Small Voice
Curtain for a Jester
Dead as a Dinosaur
Murder Comes First
The Dishonest Murderer

Murder Is Served
Untidy Murder
Death of a Tall Man
Murder Within Murder
Payoff for the Banker
Killing the Goose
Death Takes a Bow
Hanged for a Sheep
Death on the Aisle
Murder Out of Turn
A Pinch of Poison
The Norths Meet Murder
Murder in a Hurry

CAPTAIN HEIMRICH

The Distant Clue
First Come, First Kill
—With One Stone
Show Red for Danger
Accent on Murder
Practice to Deceive
Let Dead Enough Alone
Burnt Offering

Death and the Gentle Bull
Stand Up and Die
Death by Association
A Client Is Canceled
Foggy, Foggy Death
Spin Your Web, Lady
I Want to Come Home
Think of Death

MYSTERY ADVENTURES

The Devious Ones
Quest of the Bogeyman
Night of Shadows
The Ticking Clock
And Left for Dead
The Drill Is Death

The Golden Man
Murder and Blueberry Pie
The Innocent House
Catch as Catch Can
The Tangled Cord
The Faceless Adversary

CATS
Cats and People

THE
OLD
DIE
YOUNG

Richard
Lockridge

Lippincott & Crowell, Publishers
NEW YORK

FIRST EDITION

Designed by Vikki Sheatsley

Library of Congress Cataloging in Publication Data

Lockridge, Richard, 1898–
   The old die young.
   I. Title.
PZ4.L8194Ol   1980   [PS3523.O245]   813'.52   80-7775
ISBN 0-690-01948-3

80 81 82 83 84 10 9 8 7 6 5 4 3 2 1

FOR HILDY

and

FOR GEORGE STEVENS,

best of editors and friends

THE OLD DIE YOUNG

1

There were two telephones on the not-large desk in the small office. One of them was black and had been there for years. When it wanted attention it screamed. The other, the red one, had been there only about a week, and merely muttered. It was a direct-line telephone with its own number, available from outside—direct, but actually one of two extensions. The other extension was on the desk of Captain William Weigand, commanding. But Weigand was not in his office at a few minutes before noon that Monday in late September.

Nathan picked up the telephone which had muttered its summons and said "Shapiro" into it. His tone was resigned; after all, it was Monday morning.

The answer was in a woman's voice. A faintly familiar voice, but one which Lieutenant Shapiro could not immediately place. "Good morning, Nathan," whoever it was said. "I was trying to get Bill."

Of course. He should have recognized the softly pleasant voice.

"The captain isn't in today, Mrs. Weigand," Nathan Shapiro said. "Down at headquarters. The Commissioner sent for him."

"Dear old Coxey," Dorian Weigand said. It was not the way Shapiro would have referred to Edwin James Coxe, Police Commissioner of the City of New York. Of course, Mrs. Wei-

1

gand was not on the force, except by marriage. And Coxe, who had come up through the ranks, a feat just short of unique, had been Bill Weigand's first commanding officer, years ago. When Weigand had been in the uniformed division, his law studies at Columbia University interrupted by lack of funds. The Weigands and the Coxes presumably were friends, privately, hence the "dear old Coxey."

"It's like him to tell Bill himself, instead of through channels," Dorian said.

That needed no amplification. It was already well known. William Weigand had gone up from captain to deputy inspector. This meant that he would no longer command Homicide, Manhattan South, which rated nothing higher than a captain. It meant that some other captain would command the squad, of which Shapiro was one of three lieutenants. The event did nothing to brighten a Monday morning. With Bill Weigand, Nathan knew where he was. Usually, of course, in surroundings with which he was totally unfamiliar. But Nathan had got used to that. Also, he and Weigand were friends.

"Probably," Nathan told Dorian Hunt Weigand, "the captain will call in before long. Shall I tell him you called? Or, if it's urgent, you can probably reach him at the Commissioner's office."

"I don't know if it's urgent," Dorian said. "It's only—well, I feel something strange is going on."

Shapiro's life, like that of any other policeman, is largely made up of strange things going on. He said, "Something we'd be interested in, Mrs. Weigand?"

"I don't know. I think—well, I think it might be. Of course, Mr. Branson may merely have passed out, I suppose. But it would be rather a long passout, and his dresser keeps trying to wake him up and can't."

"His what?"

2

"Dresser. Helps him change. That sort of thing. It's Clive Branson, Nathan. The actor."

"You're at a theater, Mrs. Weigand?"

"No. At Mr. Branson's house. In Murray Hill. It's a house he's leased, apparently. And the dresser—Edgar Lord, his name is—lives here too. Gets Branson's meals. That sort of thing. Probably thinks of himself as a gentleman's gentleman. If the English still think that way. Or ever did, of course, except in Wodehouse. Mr. Branson's valet is what it comes to, I suppose. Dresser in the theater; valet at home. Anyway, if it's a passout, it seems to be a very long one. The party was over at about two at the latest, Lord thinks. And now it's—what time is it, Nathan?"

"Ten of twelve."

"Then I've been here two hours. My appointment was for ten and I was a few minutes early."

"Appointment?"

"To do sketches. Preliminary ones. To—oh, get the feel of him. The general shape of him, if you know what I mean."

Lieutenant Nathan Shapiro, Homicide South, was not sure he did. He did know that Dorian Weigand did sketches, sometimes caricatures. That some of them showed up in magazines. They were signed "Hunt," which had been Dorian's name before she married Captain—no, Deputy Inspector William Weigand.

"For the *Chronicle*," Dorian said. "A strip for the Arts and Leisure section. The cast of *Summer Solstice*. All four of them. Maybe the other three in a sort of circle around Branson. If it works out that way. If Branson has anything I can hang him on. Like the President's teeth, you know. Or Nixon's nose. But I won't know until I've looked at him, which was what I came down here to do. Only he won't wake up."

"Down where, Mrs. Weigand?"

"Murray Hill." She gave him an address in the mid-Thirties,

3

East Side. "It's a big old town house, not converted."

"And this dresser, this man named Lord, has been trying for two hours to wake this Branson up? This actor?"

"A very celebrated actor, Nathan. Yes. Oh, at first after he let me in, Lord said Mr. Branson would be down right away; that he was sure Mr. Branson hadn't forgotten I was coming. But after about ten minutes, he said he would go up and tell Branson I was there. He—the valet, I mean—came back in a few minutes and said Mr. Branson was having his coffee and would be right down. He said, 'I knocked at his door and he answered me. At least I'm pretty sure—' And then he asked if he couldn't bring me coffee. Or tea, perhaps. I told him no. I think he was going to say he was pretty sure Branson had answered him and decided not to. Then he went back upstairs and I got my sketch pad out and—oh, checked the light. And twiddled my thumbs. For half an hour, almost. And then Lord came to the head of the stairs and called down that Mr. Branson wasn't really wide awake yet and that maybe I'd better postpone everything. Call Miss Abel and set up another date.

"Miss Abel?"

"Branson's agent. The one I talked to after the *Chronicle* decided it wanted the spread; thought probably *Summer Solstice* would run that long, anyway. And they'd pretty much promised Simon's publicity man."

"Simon?"

Dorian Weigand kept tossing bits and pieces at him, which, he thought, was not like her. Although, after all, he didn't know her that well. She was evidently having an upsetting morning.

She was sorry, she said. Probably she wasn't tracking too well. Rolf Simon, producer of a play called *Summer Solstice,* by Bret Askew, which had opened two weeks before. "To mixed notices," Dorian added. "Although it was supposed to be a smash.

4

Branson's the star. I keep feeling somebody ought to do something about him right now, although of course it's not my business. Or yours. I just—well, wanted to talk to Bill about it. Because it doesn't feel right."

It was beginning not to feel right to Shapiro.

"This man Lord," Shapiro said. "Maybe he ought to call Branson's doctor."

"I suggested that, Nathan. Lord doesn't think Mr.—he's heavy on the 'mister'—Branson has a doctor. Not in New York, anyway. Maybe on the West Coast. But he doubts it. Mr. Branson is never sick. Lord never knew him to be. 'Not in all the years I've been with him,' he said. So I suggested he call for an ambulance because—well, people don't sleep all this soundly, do they? Lord has been calling his name. Rather loudly the last few minutes. And—well, shaking him, I think. Putting cold water on his head. I don't know what all."

"And Lord doesn't want to call an ambulance?"

"Says, 'Oh, Mr. Branson wouldn't want me to do *that!*'" Her emphasis was heavy on the word "that," as presumably Lord's had been.

"Did he say why, Mrs. Weigand? Why Mr. Branson wouldn't want an ambulance called?"

"No. Probably it is more the way Lord feels himself. Very protective, Lord seems to be. And fuddy-duddy. Doesn't want outsiders intruding. Did I tell you Lord sounds rather English? In accent, I mean."

She had not. "Is there anyone else there, Mrs. Weigand? Servants or something?"

"Just the dresser and me, far's I know. And I feel—well, responsible. Which is absurd, of course. Still—somebody ought to do something. So, I called Bill."

"And got me instead." He paused. Probably nothing for the

5

police to get involved in. A protracted passout. Or possibly a heart attack, of course. Not a concern of Manhattan South. Still, he didn't think Dorian Weigand would make mountains of molehills.

"This party last night," Shapiro said. "This man Lord say how late it lasted?"

"He doesn't know. Says he doesn't. Says he went up to his room—he stays on the top floor—about eleven. Says Mr. Branson told him to. Seems it was a surprise party. Birthday party for Branson. The people giving it—Mr. Simon chiefly, Lord thinks—brought in waiters. Bartender, anyway. And provided the drinks and whatever food they had. The party started about ten, Lord says. When he started to let people in."

"This man Simon. The producer. Who else does Lord say?"

"Pretty much the whole cast of *Summer Solstice,* apparently. Nathan, we've got to do something."

"Yes," Nathan Shapiro said. "I'll put in a call for an ambulance. And tell the cap—the deputy inspector—when he comes in. And you? You want to stay there?"

"Not much. But I can. I will."

Nathan put in the call. Through channels, which would bring not only an ambulance, probably from Bellevue, but also a patrol car from precinct. For a man who didn't want either. Who probably wanted to be left alone to sleep off a hangover.

After he had made the call, Lieutenant Shapiro looked fixedly at the two telephones on his desk; then, abruptly, he stood up and went out through the squad room. Tony Cook, detective (1st gr.), was at a desk. He was typing. But when Shapiro, with a movement of the head, summoned him, Tony Cook quit typing.

2

There was a dignified defiance, Shapiro thought, about the old town house. It stood in mid-block, was four stories tall and was made of brick, which had been painted white—rather recently painted white. Bricks age in a hundred years or so. The house stood a little withdrawn from apartment houses towering over it on either side. Once, undoubtedly, it had stood shoulder to shoulder with other houses like itself, forming a block-long wall of dignity. Farther up the block, another survivor of its kind still stood, but it was more worn. It too was of brick, but many summer and winter storms had eroded it.

The half-dozen steps leading up to the front door of the white-brick house were of sandstone, scrubbed clean and a little worn by many feet. The brass rails on the sides of the short staircase were highly polished. The steps leading down from the sidewalk ended at the entryway of the bottom floor. The floor would be a basement in the front of the house, but in the rear would open on a back yard which almost certainly was called a "garden."

Shapiro and Tony Cook climbed the steps to double front doors. Shapiro pressed the bell push. A bell sounded beyond the double doors. It was a bell, not chimes. The old house would have no truck with fripperies.

They waited for a long time. Then one of the doors opened and a man stood in the doorway. He was tall and thin and, sparsely, gray-haired. He wore a black suit and a stiff white collar with a black string tie. He said, "Yes, gentlemen?"

He sounded English, all right. It occurred to Shapiro that he should have been wearing a wing collar. But Rose and Nathan Shapiro had been watching "Upstairs, Downstairs" on television.

"Mr. Branson?" Shapiro said.

"I am afraid Mr. Branson is occupied," Edgar Lord said. "If you would care to leave your cards, gentlemen?"

"Then," Shapiro said, "Mrs. Weigand, if she is still here."

Lord raised gray and somewhat bristling eyebrows.

"Miss Hunt," Shapiro said. "The artist who's here to do sketches of Mr. Branson. Is she still around, Mr. Lord?"

Lord hesitated for a moment as if he were consulting himself. Then he said, "Probably the lady has left. She was about to when I took coffee up to Mr. Branson."

"Make sure she has, please," Shapiro said, suiting his idiom to the dark-suited man's. "And tell her Lieutenant Shapiro would like to see her."

Lord said, "Lieutenant?" with doubt in his voice, a doubt Nathan Shapiro could understand and even share.

"Police lieutenant," Shapiro said.

Lord said, "Sir," and drew back and started to close the door. Shapiro prepared to place a foot in it, but from behind the butler-valet-dresser, Dorian Weigand said, "Nathan!" and then, "Did you?"

"Yes," Shapiro said. "Ought to be here any time. By now, actually."

A siren, still several blocks away, took up its cue. A second siren joined it.

"Mr. Branson will be displeased," Lord said. "He does not like invasions of his privacy." But he stepped back from the

8

door, leaving it open. Shapiro and Cook went into the house—into a rather narrow entrance hall with a staircase rising out of it.

Dorian stood in a doorway on their right. Shapiro had almost forgotten how green her eyes were. She moved toward him. He had almost forgotten how lightly she moved, how much with the grace of a cat.

"I'm glad you called them," she said. "But I didn't expect you to come yourself."

"Thought I might as well," Nathan said. "Quiet morning, anyway. You know Detective Cook, don't you?"

Dorian did. She had met Tony Cook when a painter was murdered a few years back. (When she had also met Shapiro; when she had almost been pushed under a bus.)

She said, "Good morning, Mr. Cook," and, "I'm afraid I—" But then a siren made a dying moan outside and Shapiro opened the door, to which Lord paid no attention. The ambulance was from Bellevue. The cruise car which nosed up behind it was from precinct. Two young men in white got out of the ambulance and withdrew a stretcher from it. A uniformed policeman got out of the police car, leaving another uniformed policeman in it. The three came up the immaculate steps.

"You the one wanted an ambulance?" the patrolman asked. Shapiro said, "Yes," and took his gold shield out of a jacket pocket and showed it. The patrolman said, "Sir," and turned to beckon to the other uniformed man, who got out from behind the wheel and came to join them.

"Where?" Shapiro said to Edgar Lord.

"Upstairs," Lord said. "But I don't know whether—"

"Your patient's upstairs," Shapiro told the ambulance men. "Mr. Lord here will show you. Name of Branson. Mr. Lord hasn't been able to wake him up."

9

One of the ambulance men said, "O.K.," and looked at the badge still cupped in Shapiro's hand and added, "Lieutenant."

Lord shrugged narrow shoulders and seemed about to say something. But he did not; he merely shrugged his shoulders again, in evident resignation. Then he went up the stairs from the entrance hall, and the men in white went after him, carrying the folded stretcher. Shapiro watched the climb. The flight was rather long. Old town houses have high ceilings. At the top, Lord led them along a hallway toward the rear of the house.

"We may as well sit down, I guess," Dorian Weigand said, and turned back to the doorway she had come through.

The room into which they followed her was wide; except for the entrance hall, the width of the house. It was also deep. At the far end there were glass doors opening on a terrace, with sunlight falling on it. The light fell also on a small, neat stack of firewood, waiting for autumn and winter fires in the fireplace in the long wall of the living room—no, the drawing room. It would have been called that when the old house was young.

There was a long sofa facing the fireplace, which was small and held a basket, not fire irons. Coal, not wood, had been burned in the fireplace when it heated—partly heated—the big room. Dorian Weigand went to sit on the sofa, and Shapiro sat beside her. Tony Cook leaned against the wall near the door from the hall.

"Probably," Dorian said, "I've just caused everybody a lot of trouble. Just blundered in and made a mess of things. Bill won't like it."

"You had a right to wonder," Shapiro told her. "People don't usually pass out for this long. This man Lord doesn't know what time the party, the surprise birthday party, ended?"

"What he says. He let people in from around ten o'clock on. It was about eleven, he thinks, when Mr. Branson told him he

10

might as well go up to bed. And he did go. The party was just getting started when he went."

"Where is Lord's room, did he say?"

"The top floor."

"That would be the fourth," Shapiro said. "Went up and went to sleep? The party—in this room, I suppose—didn't keep him awake?"

She didn't know. "Most of the time I've been here, Mr. Lord has been upstairs, trying to waken his master. At least I suppose that's what Lord calls him. Although it was 'Mr. Branson' to me."

"Probably," Shapiro said, and thought again of butlers with stiff wing collars. "Did Lord say what birthday this was of Branson's?"

Lord had not. In the play, Branson was a man in his early forties, married to a woman barely in her twenties. "But he seemed a little—"

She did not finish, but turned to look toward the door to the hall. Shapiro turned too.

"It's a DOA, Lieutenant," the ambulance man said from the doorway. "A couple of hours ago, anyway. Want we should—"

"No," Shapiro said. "I'm afraid it's a suspicious death as of now."

"Could be just his heart," the ambulance man said. "Or it could be anything, I guess. Not shot or stabbed or anything like that. Just went out peacefully, looks like. One funny thing, he doesn't really look dead—not the way they do usually. First looked at him, Ned and I thought he was still alive. Only he wasn't. Like I said, dead a couple of hours, anyway. Pretty much cooled off."

Dorian said, "Oh," and turned to look at the fireplace, which was also cold.

11

"Yes," Shapiro said. "You two may as well report in. And if he's still outside, tell the sergeant to come in, will you?"

The ambulance man would, and did. Shapiro took his badge out of his pocket and fastened it to his jacket, as rules and regulations stipulated when at the scene of a crime. If, of couse, he was.

The uniformed sergeant came in. He said, "Sergeant O'Brien, Lieutenant. No patient?"

"Not alive," Shapiro told him. "A Mr. Branson. A Mr.—what Branson, Mrs. Weigand?"

"Clive," Dorian said. "That would have upset him, Nathan. Everybody is supposed to have heard of Clive Branson. On the tip of everybody's tongue, it's supposed to be."

"I don't know much about the theater," Shapiro said. "Clive Branson, O'Brien. An actor."

"The Clive Branson, sir," the sergeant said. "Pretty—well, famous, sir."

"All right, sergeant. For your report, Clive Branson, actor. DOA. Suspicious death. Who heads up the squad at your precinct?"

Each precinct station house of the New York Police Department has its own detective squad.

"Captain Digby, Lieutenant. Acting captain, that is."

"I'm Shapiro, Homicide South. Pass the word to him. Tell him, or whoever's catching, that I—well, just happened to be here. And am standing in." The homicide squads of greater New York wait to be called in when things get sticky. Shapiro's presence was mildly irregular. O'Brien said, "Sir," supplying formality, and went out to collect his car partner and call in.

Shapiro found a telephone and called in himself, reporting a suspicious death and the need for an assistant medical examiner

12

and the morgue van. Photographers and technicians would come from precinct.

"You don't need me anymore," Dorian told him. "Suppose I—well, call somebody, Miss Abel, I guess, and break the news. His agent, Martha Abel is. Tell her there won't be any sketch and that her percentage is dead."

"Yes, Mrs. Weigand," Shapiro said, in the voice of one who is thinking of something else. "That'll be fine, be a help."

"And," Dorian said, "that *Summer Solstice* won't be playing tonight. At least, I suppose it won't. Period of mourning before the understudy takes over. If Mr. Simon feels in a sentimental mood."

"Yes," Shapiro said, in the same absent voice. "Tony, you want to get Mrs. Weigand a taxi?"

Tony Cook was told by Dorian that he didn't need to, that she could get a cab herself. Tony went out to get a cab and didn't have any trouble—not any real trouble, anyway.

Nathan Shapiro climbed the long flight of rather narrow stairs to have a look at a dead man who, in some fashion not spelled out, didn't really look dead to a man who, in his daily work, saw a good many men and women who did.

3

The bedroom of the late Clive Branson was at the rear end of a long hallway on the second floor. It was a high-ceilinged room, and the windows were tall, almost from floor to ceiling. They overlooked the garden, in which a few flowers were still blooming.

Edgar Lord sat in a straight chair facing one of the windows. There were easy chairs facing the same way, but Lord had chosen the straightest. He sat with his back to a wide bed and was looking down at the garden. He had turned slowly when Shapiro and Cook opened the closed door and went into the room. Then he stood up, shoulders stiffened. He said, "Sir?" in a tone of doubt. Then he said, "Is there something you'd like, sir?" to Nathan Shapiro.

It was clear to Nathan what Lord would like. He would like them to go away, to cease intruding on Mr. Branson's bedroom. (Bed*chamber*?)

"We just have to look around, Mr. Lord," Shapiro said. "Sudden and unexpected death has to—well, has to be looked into, you know."

"I presume so," Lord said. "Although—" He did not finish. He remained standing. He did not look at the dead man lying face up in the middle of a wide bed.

Branson had been wearing dark-blue pajamas when he died.

14

In an ashtray by the bed he had stubbed out two cigarettes. One butt was considerably longer than the other and had bent in the fingers which crushed it out, as if it had been extinguished quickly, rather fumblingly.

Lord saw the ashtray when Shapiro did and said, "I'm sorry, sir," and reached toward the tray.

"No, Mr. Lord," Shapiro said. "You can straighten up later. After we've finished. There'll be a police photographer along. And a physician. And—well, a few others. Tell you what, you might go down and see that they get in. All right?"

"Very well, sir. Will these other gentlemen be in uniform?"

"One or two may. The others will have badges. There may be reporters later. But the patrolmen will take care of them."

"Very well, Lieutenant." Lord's voice grew a little brighter with that. It was for him, Shapiro thought, as if things were reverting to the normal, to the to-be-expected. When Lord went out he closed the door after him, closed it with careful quiet.

Shapiro leaned down and looked at the body of Clive Branson. It looked peaceful enough. But there was something which did not look as it would be expected to look. The something, Shapiro thought, the ambulance man had meant when he had said that the man did not quite look dead. What the ambulance man had seen was not immediately apparent. Shapiro touched the smooth, almost unlined forehead. It was cold to the touch.

The answer came slowly. The face he bent over did not have the unmistakable pallor of death. Warm blood did not circulate in the cold skin of the forehead, and yet there, as in the smoothly shaven cheeks, there remained the tint of life. Again Shapiro touched the cold forehead. He rubbed it gently. He examined his own fingertips; walked to the windows, where the light was better.

It was hard to be certain, but it seemed to him that the tips of

15

his fingers were just perceptibly colored. He rubbed his finger-tips together. They were faintly slippery.

Tony Cook was watching him. He looked at Tony.

"Yes," Tony said. "What I thought too. He's wearing make-up. And look at his hair, Nate. The roots of his hair."

Shapiro had noticed the deep-brown, professionally styled hair of the dead man. He looked more closely, being now sure enough what he would find. The roots of the hair were gray.

"And," Tony said, "a face lift, wouldn't you say?"

The surgeon had been as expert as the hair stylist, as the person who had dyed Clive Branson's hair. The scars left by the surgeon's scapel were almost invisible.

"We'd better get the dresser back up, Tony," Shapiro said. "Maybe he can tell us a little more about Branson. How old he really was, for example."

Tony went down the long hall and down the narrow, rather steep stairs to get Edgar Lord, dresser, valet, and, apparently, butler also. The uniformed men from the cruise car would see that the asssitant medical examiner and the technical men from precinct and the lab got in all right and were told where their jobs were.

But when Tony Cook came back to the bedroom, it was not with Lord. He guided a small, neat man in a trim blue suit. The man was carrying a black bag.

He said, "Doctor Nelson, Lietenant. M.E.'s office. Suspicious death?"

"To me it is," Shapiro said. "Could be just heart failure, I suppose."

"Cardiac arrest," Dr. Nelson said. He touched the cold fore-head. He pulled back the light coverlet and lifted the right arm. "Rigor setting in," he said. "Heart stopped several hours ago,

16

I'd say. Have to open him up to be sure. The van will be along. O.K.?"

"When we finish with it," Shapiro told him.

"The gang's downstairs," Tony said. "Starting on the living room where this birthday party was. And the photographer's ready to start shooting up here."

"Yes," Shapiro said. "We'll get out from underfoot, Tony. Have a little talk with Mr. Lord somewhere else. You might ask him where."

Lord didn't know what he could tell them that he hadn't already told. But as they wished, of course. Perhaps his room? If they didn't mind the stairs.

They didn't mind the stairs. Lord's room was on the top floor—the fourth. It was also at the rear of the building and had windows overlooking the garden. These windows were much smaller; the ceiling of this room was much lower. Lord's bed was narrow; it was neatly made up. There were two chairs in the room, one straight, the other cushioned. Not very deeply cushioned, Shapiro guessed. He motioned Lord to sit in it. Lord said, "Sir?"

"It's your room," Shapiro said and sat on the straight chair, which had a hard wooden seat. Cook closed the door and stood by it and took out his notebook.

"Now," Shapiro said, "tell us about last night, Mr. Lord. About this party, to start with. It was a surprise birthday party, I understand."

"I wasn't actually at it, sir. My services were—well, not needed. Mr. Branson told me to come up here. 'Go up and get some sleep,' was what he said. He's—he was a very considerate gentleman, Lieutenant. And they had a man with them to mix drinks and another man, from some catering firm, I gathered,

17

with food. Sandwiches, mostly, I think. There were a few left when I straightened up this morning."

He had found a plate with a few sandwiches on it; glasses, washed and neatly stacked on a tray. Little straightening up left for him to do.

"The glasses had been washed? And what kind of glasses?"

"Washed and polished, sir. Highball glasses and wine glasses. Champagne, I assume. There were two champagne bottles in the dust bin. Taittinger. I presume they toasted Mr. Branson on his birthday."

"Yes," Shapiro said. "Who would 'they' have been, do you know? Did you let them all in, Mr. Lord?"

"I think so. Others may have come after I retired, I suppose. I let in the other members of the cast—there are only four in the cast of *Summer Solstice,* sir—and the playwright, Mr. Bret Askew. And the director. Almost everybody connected with the production, Lieutenant. And Miss Abel. She's Mr. Branson's agent, you know. What they call an artists' representative."

"Do they, Lord? I'm afraid I'm not very familiar with these matters."

There was mournful resignation in Nathan Shapiro's voice. Tony Cook recognized it. Nate, once more, thought he was out of his depth in a strange swamp.

"Quite a gathering," Shapiro said. "And this celebration really came as a surprise to Mr. Branson? Nobody—well, leaked it in advance? People do, sometimes."

"I believe it was entirely a surprise to him, sir. If he had had any inkling he would have alerted me, I'm quite certain. As I said, he was a very considerate employer, Lieutenant."

"Speaking of that, Mr. Lord, how long had he been your employer?"

"Ten years, sir. He engaged me in London, when he was

18

playing Hamlet. The critics were most enthusiastic. Better than Olivier, one of them said. Particularly in the scene with his mother."

Shapiro nodded, indicating that he at least knew who Olivier was. Hamlet too, for that matter. "Very gratifying to Mr. Branson, that must have been. And you came over here with him, and have been with him ever since?"

"To the States, yes, Lieutenant. Several years in Hollywood, of course. Very successful in the flicks, he was. In the cinema, that is. We came east last spring. Rehearsed during the summer. It was very warm here during the past summer, we both thought."

"I was here during the summer, Mr. Lord. It was *hot*. Did Mr. Branson much mind the heat, did he say?"

"He didn't complain about it. Not to me, anyway. But he wouldn't have, would he, sir? To his dresser, that is."

Shapiro didn't know. He said, "Probably not," and then, "How old was Mr. Branson, Mr. Lord?"

Shapiro saw the thin man in the dark suit swallow. The swallow seemed to prevent an immediate answer. Shapiro waited.

"Early forties, I believe, sir. He never mentioned his age to me. It would be in *Who's Who*, sir. *Who's Who in the Theatre,* certainly."

"About the age I'd have guessed from looking at him," Shapiro said. "Or—about the age he was made up to look. Did you help him with the makeup, Lord?"

Lord said, "Makeup, sir?" as if the word were one he had never heard before.

Shapiro merely looked at him for a moment, then said, "The makeup he was wearing when he died."

Lord did not know what the lieutenant meant. Mr. Branson wore makeup on the stage, of course. All actors do. Lord had

19

never helped him with the stage makeup. He had always applied that himself, except in Hollywood, where they had experts to do that sort of thing—for the stars, at any rate. So far as Lord knew, Mr. Branson never used makeup offstage. Why should he?

"Possibly to make himself appear younger," Shapiro said. "To be in the early forties, as you think he was. As probably *Who's Who* will confirm he was. I understand it accepts whatever it is told—told by the subjects of the articles."

"To make himself look younger, sir?"

"The age of the character in the play," Shapiro said. "A youngish man married to a much younger woman. Isn't that true in *Summer Solstice,* Mr. Lord?"

Lord merely nodded.

"Mr. Branson was in good health as far as you know? Nothing, say, the matter with his heart?"

"He played tennis a good deal during the summer," Lord said. "And squash in the winter. If he had a tricky heart, he wouldn't have done that, would he, sir?"

"I wouldn't think so," Shapiro said. "If he knew about it, of course. Do you know whether he'd been seeing a doctor?"

Not that Lord knew of. Yes, he supposed he would have known. Oh, when they had been on the West Coast, Mr. Branson had seen a doctor once or twice. About an allergy, Lord thought.

Not, apparently, any ailment which would cause a man to die in his sleep. Whatever that might be. There again Shapiro could claim no real knowledge.

"Do you happen to know whether he took sleeping medicine, Mr. Lord? Barbiturates or anything like that?"

That Lord did know. Branson had never taken sleeping pills. "He had an overreaction to the barbiturates, he told me once. He said he had found out when he was still very young. That was all he said."

"Overreactive," Shapiro said. "That comes out as death from unknown causes. Which makes it what we call a suspicious death. Which means there will have to be an autopsy. Mr. Branson wasn't married, I take it?"

"I believe he had been, sir. When he was young, I believe. Before he employed me, certainly."

"Any close relatives? Sisters, brothers?"

"I believe not, Lieutenant. At least, he never mentioned any relatives to me. Who would have to agree to a postmortem examination, you mean, sir?"

"Not agree to, Lord. It's required by law. To be told about. As a matter of courtesy, you might say."

"I know of no one, sir. I believe Mr. Branson was quite alone. Except for me, you might say, sir." And his voice seemed to break a little.

"Nobody to notify of his death, then?"

Not as far as he—oh, his agent, Lord supposed. Miss Abel, that would be. Martha Abel. Martha Abel Associates. Oh, and Mr. Simon, of course. Rolf Simon, the producer of *Summer Solstice*. Should he—?

"Mrs. Weig—Miss Hunt was going to call Miss Abel," Shapiro told him, "but we will want to talk to her. Martha Abel Associates, you say? Office in New York, Mr. Lord?"

There were offices both in New York and in Los Angeles. Martha Abel herself, Lord thought, was usually in New York.

There was, faintly, the sound of movement below them. Tony Cook opened the door.

"Taking it away, sounds like," Tony said. "Guess they've finished up in the bedroom."

"It" would be the body of Clive Branson, actor. "They"

would be the photographer, the fingerprint men, the man who had made a sketch of the bedroom, locating bed and chairs and chest of drawers with mirror over it. The mirror Branson had sat in front of when he applied light makeup to his handsome face, carefully adjusted his abundant, deep-brown hair? Presumably.

In half an hour, Branson's body would be on an autopsy table, and gloved men in white would be at it with scalpels and with saws. Specimens of it would be placed in sterile flasks. The body would have been measured and weighed and its age estimated; makeup would be scraped from the face for analysis.

But there might, of course, be cadavers ahead of it. This was Monday, after all, and cadavers accumulate on weekends. On weekends, people are off jobs and hence free to kill their fellows.

"Detective Cook will draw up what you've told us as a statement," Shapiro told Edgar Lord. "We'll ask you to sign it. This evening, perhaps; or perhaps not until tomorrow. You'll be here, Mr. Lord?"

"Certainly, sir." Lord said.

Detectives and technicians were still at work in the big living-drawing room on the ground—all right, the entrance floor, since it was considerably above ground level, up scrubbed steps from the sidewalk.

4

Martha Abel Associates was listed in the Manhattan telephone directory. The address was in the West Fifties, easy walking distance from "21," which would provide lunch convenience for staff and clients, if clients were usually of the apparent stature of the late Clive Branson.

Martha Abel must be talked to, although Dorian Weigand would already have broken the news to her—or an associate—of Branson's death.

The squad car which had brought Shapiro and Cook from Manhattan South had gone back there. They took a cab to the West Fifties.

The office building was elderly and dignified and only five stories tall. Martha Abel Associates occupied the top floor. The waiting room had comfortable chairs for waiters, of which there were none. A pretty young woman at a desk was using the telephone. She said, "All right, darling, if you say he's super he's super," into the telephone and cradled it. She looked up at Nathan Shapiro and said, "Yes? May I help you?"

Shapiro said, "Miss Abel, please." He was asked if he had an appointment. He identified himself, and the pretty young woman said, "Oh."

"About Mr. Branson," Shapiro said, and this time she said, "Oh, dear." But she used the telephone and said that a policeman was there about Mr. Branson. Then she said, "Of course, Mrs. Abel," and stood up. If the lieutenant, she said, would just come this way. . . .

Miss Abel sat with her back to a window at an uncluttered desk at the far end of a deeply carpeted room. She watched Shapiro as he walked the length of the room, with Tony Cook a little behind him. When he was a step or two from her, she stood up behind the desk. She was a white-haired woman, prematurely white-haired, Shapiro thought. The rest of her appeared to be in the mid-thirties, and she was almost beautiful.

She said, "About poor dear Clive, but why the police?"

"Because we don't know the cause of Mr. Branson's sudden death," Shapiro told her. "And there seems to be no doctor to sign a certificate. So we have to look into things. We're from Homicide, Miss Abel."

"And you think somebody killed Clive? Somebody at the party last night? By putting poison in his drink? That's absurd, Lieutenant—Shapiro. That's right, isn't it? Shapiro?"

Shapiro told her that was right. He said, "Absurd, Miss Abel?"

"Of course. Clive was such a sweet man. Why would anybody want to?"

"Kill him? I've no idea. And it's not at all clear anybody did. It's just a possibility we have to rule out. Or in. I understand you were at this party, Miss Abel. This birthday surprise party?"

"Yes. Mr. Simon set it up, actually. Arranged everything. Getting Clive in his play was—well, what they call a feather in his cap, you know. Would have been in any producer's. And the advance sale! Really, Lieutenant. And what will happen now, God knows. It's—it's a catastrophe."

"You mean, Mr. Simon will have to close the play?"

She had continued to stand behind her desk. Now she sat

down behind it. She looked down at the desk top. When she spoke, she spoke slowly. "I don't know," she said. "I really don't know. They may try to keep it running with Ken Price. He's the understudy—besides having the other male role. He's good. He's very good. But—well, people went to see Clive. More him than Bret Askew's play. Not that it isn't a very nice little play, but it was Clive they've been coming to see. And buying advance tickets to see. They'll get a lot of cancellations, I'm afraid. And after only two weeks! Why, it might have run for two years. And now . . ."

Shapiro made what he hoped was a sound of sympathy. He said, "About this party last night, Miss Abel. About what time—"

He was interrupted. The door to Martha Abel's office opened, and a man's voice said, "*Darling.* I—"

The man who followed the voice into the office was tall and noticeably handsome. He was, at a guess, in his late thirties. Vaguely, he reminded Shapiro of someone he had seen, and seen recently. Oh, yes, of a dead man. Not strikingly; this man was much younger. But he had somewhat the same actor's face, the same definition of features. And an actor's voice.

The handsome youngish man stopped just inside the door; stopped, obviously, when he saw Shapiro and Tony Cook.

"I say," he said. "I am sorry, Miss Abel. Gracie's taking a coffee break or something. Didn't realize you were busy. So I just barged—"

"It's all right, Ken," said "Darling"—or, alternatively, Martha Abel. "They're from the police. About poor dear Clive."

"The police?" Ken said, with an inflection of entire disbelief. "Why on earth the police?"

"This is Kenneth Price, Lieutenant," the white-haired talent agent said. "The man who'll take over poor Mr. Branson's role if Mr. Simon decides to keep *Solstice* open."

"What I came to tell you about," Price said. "Not tonight, but tomorrow night, looks like. With me in Clive's part. Money refunded on demand, of course, to last-ditch Clive Branson fans. It's too damm bad about old Clive. Swell guy and great professional. I couldn't be sorrier. But how do the cops come into it? Clive just died, didn't he?"

This last seemed directed to Shapiro or Tony Cook. Shapiro identified himself and Tony to Price, then said, "He died in his sleep, apparently. We have to try to find out why, Mr. Price. Apparently he was in good health. Hadn't been seeing a doctor, far's we can make out. So—routine inquiry."

"On the chance somebody killed Clive, Lieutenant? Way-out notion, I'd think."

"Very possibly," Shapiro said.

"Hey," Price said. You don't think somebody at this damn party—well, put cyanide in his drink?"

"No, not cyanide, Mr. Price. Probably nothing. The P.M. will tell us about that. The autopsy."

"Jeez!" Price said. "The old boy would hate that. So—well, careful of himself, the old boy was."

"Don't be so flip," Martha Abel said. "You're not playing comedy."

"Sorry, darling," Price said, in a different tone. "Bad reaction to Clive's death. So—sudden; so needless. Hell, he and I had a tennis date for this afternoon. I'm sort of knocked for a loop, I guess. Brings out the ham in me, apparently. Sorry about it."

"It's all right, dear," Martha Abel said. "I'm sure the lieutenant understands."

"Everybody gets edgy with a thing like this," Shapiro told them both. "You were at this birthday party last night, Mr. Price? Why 'damn' party, by the way?"

26

"Sure, we all were. Producer, author, cast. I don't know why I said 'damn' party, Lieutenant. Actually, it was a very good party. Good drinks, all-right food, good people. Even Kirby."

"Bob Kirby directed the play," Martha said. "And he usually stays clear of parties."

Shapiro said he saw. It was something he seemed to himself to be always saying, whether it was true or not. He said he was interested in the party. Had it been planned long? Who had planned it?

"Mr. Simon planned it," Martha Abel said. "Do sit down somewhere, Ken. Don't just stand there glowering."

"Didn't know I was, darling," Price said. But he pulled a light chair nearer an end of the desk and sat on it.

"Or Rolf Simon's secretary, probably," Martha Abel said. "Very efficient gal. She called me Friday, I think it was, and told me about it. Friday morning. Called you about the same time, I suppose, Ken?"

"Afternoon," Price said. "Yes, Friday."

"Said we seemed to be off to a flying start, and that Mr. Simon thought it called for a little celebration. Figured Clive had it coming on his birthday."

Everybody seemed to know the birthday of the late Clive Branson, and nobody seemed to know how old Branson had been on the last evening of his life. Did Price know?"

"Probably in *Who's Who in the Theatre*," Price said. "Got a copy here, haven't you, Marty?"

"Over there," Martha said, and pointed toward a small bookcase against a wall. Price went to the bookcase and took a rather thick book out of it. He flicked pages. Then he said, "Yeah," and, after a moment, "Comes out forty-two, way I figure it," he said. "I'd have thought—" He did not say what he would have thought. He put the *Who's Who,* open, on the desk in front of

Martha Abel. She merely glanced at it and closed it up. Then she said, "Forty-two it is."

"What he told them," Price said.

"Yes, Ken," she said. "What they have to go on, isn't it? All right, maybe he fudged a little. Don't we all? In the profession, we do. I suppose we do." She looked down for a moment at the top of her desk. Then she looked at Shapiro. "Acting's a physical profession. Women start off as ingenues and end up playing grandmother roles. With an interim as character actors. Men play juvenile leads, character actors, old fuddy-duddies. We— well, try to postpone the progression. Unless we get put out of it. As I did—almost before I even got into it, really. Marilyn Blake, rising young star. Only she wasn't, as it turned out. So now, actor's agent. Flesh peddler, for short. And better off."

Price said, "Sure you are, darling." Then, for several seconds, nobody said anything.

" 'Off to a flying start,' " Shapiro said. "Meaning the play, of course. It was, Miss Abel?"

"Of course. Advance sale into next year. And the notices! Raves!"

There was another silence. Price broke this one with a cough, a stage cough, Shapiro found himself thinking. He followed it with, "Look, darling, the man can read. Probably will, I suspect. Raves, Marty?"

"Damn good notices," Martha Abel said. " 'Noel Coward at his most lighthearted.' New York *Chronicle*."

"Branson is termed 'some years too old for the role' by the New York *Sentinel*," Price said. "And the *Chronicle* said that he, 'for all his competence, is still too heavy.' Raves, darling?"

"It'll run for a couple of years," Martha said. There was a warning note in her voice.

Price said, "Sure. Maybe three or four. Speaking of which—

Clive had run of the play, you know. You got him that."

"Branson was a star, Ken."

"And I'm not," Price said. "Which you won't, I hope, be pointing out to dear old Rolf, since, after all, I'm in your stable too. Not Clive's salary. All right. But run of the play, anyway. O.K., darling?"

"We'll see how it goes tomorrow night. You're up on it, aren't you?"

"Of course I'm up on it," Price said. "Lines and—"

The telephone on the desk interrupted him. Martha Abel let it ring several times. Then she said, "Damn that girl," and lifted the receiver. She said, "Martha Abel Associates," then, "Yes, it is," and listened for a moment. "Yes, happens he's right here," and listened again. Then she said, "All right, I'll send him along," and put the receiver back in its cradle.

"Kirby called a rehearsal, Ken," she said. "Simon will be there."

Ken Price stood up. He said, "Now?"

"An hour ago's more like it," his agent told him. "They've been trying to find you. So you'd better get going. You're sure you're up on the part?"

"Lines and business, darling. And you'll talk to the old boy?"

"After tomorrow night. Mr. Simon will try to get the reviewers back for it. The *Chronicle* man, anyway—there's nothing opening tomorrow. On your way, sweetheart."

Ken Price got on his way.

"Nice boy," Martha said, "And an all-right actor. Almost as good as he thinks he is. So?"

"About the party?"

"Drinks and sandwiches. And a hot dish I didn't try. And patting one another on the back. And singing happy birthday, dear Clivey, and many happy returns. *Jesus!*"

29

"Yes," Shapiro said. "For about how long, Miss Abel?"

"It's *Mrs.* Abel actually, Lieutenant. Was until a couple of years ago, anyway—two years and six months, to be precise. After ten years. Good years for the most part. But you don't want the story of my life, do you? Just of last night, right?"

Shapiro nodded.

"Ken picked me up a little before ten. At my apartment. It's in the East Sixties. Ken lives at the Algonquin—where else? We got down to Clive's house about—oh, say ten fifteen. The party was already rolling. Scotch, bourbon, and champagne. And everybody *'Darling!'*—the way they all talk. Some try for 'dahling,' like the late Miss Bankhead, and don't quite bring it off. Except for Rolf Simon. They were saying, 'So glad you could make it, Mrs. Abel.' And I said I wouldn't have missed it, and Scotch and water, please, to a waiter Mr. Simon had brought along, and I clicked with Clive and wished him many happy returns. *Jesus!*"

"Yes," Shapiro said again. "Mr. Branson was your client?"

"Why you're here, isn't it? In my stable, yes. And a friend. And a hell of an actor—all right, a few years ago, anyway. After a while, everything gets to be a few years ago, doesn't it? Stage direction: *Marilyn Blake weeps for the vanished past into a fragile handkerchief.*" She stopped and shook her head. "And I told poor Ken not to be flip," she said. "Sorry, Lieutenant. I'm—I'm, shaken up too, I guess. So Clive kissed me on both cheeks, and some more people came in and wished him many happy returns, and it went on that way."

"For about how long, Mrs. Abel?"

As far as she was concerned, until about half-past twelve, at a guess.

"I keep office hours here," she said. "So when Arlene said she was going to call it a night, I decided to too."

"Arlene?"

"Arlene Collins. Plays the female lead, opposite Clive. Or opposite Ken now, if Mr. Simon decides to keep it on. Sweet kid and an all-right actor. Better than that, actually. Had a bit part in a small stinker last season, but a couple of the critics gave her raves. Happened to Hepburn years ago. Did you know that, Lieutenant?"

"No," Shapiro said. "I'm afraid I don't know much about the theater."

"Heard of Hepburn, all the same?"

Shapiro admitted he had heard of Miss Hepburn. He said, "So you and Miss Collins left the party about half-past twelve?"

"About then, as I told you. The waiter got us a cab. I dropped her off at West Ninth and went home. She insisted on paying what was on the meter that far. Nice kid. Annie Burbaum, originally. Can't blame her for the change, can you?"

Shapiro couldn't. "Leaving how many at the party, Mrs. Abel?"

She counted on her fingers, giving a name to each finger. "Clive, of course. And Mr. Simon. And—"

Shapiro let six names tick into his memory and, presumably, out of it. Tony Cook would be getting the names down, along with their roles in the production of *Summer Solstice.*

Three of the five were actors. One was the director. Bob something. Kirby? Tony would have the rest of it in his notes. Something Askew. Bert? Tony would have it down. He was the playwright, author of *Summer Solstice.*

"Askew was with them during the tryouts," Martha Abel explained, "here in town. Got to be one of the family, pretty much. For all he kept changing the script. Nice enough kid. First time he's got to Broadway. Off a couple of times. Even off-off once, Bret was."

That was it. Bret, not Bert. So. Helen something. "Plays Carol's mother. You haven't seen the play, have you, Lieutenant? Carol's the young wife. Part Arlene plays. Married to Louis Derwent. Clive's part. Supposed to be twice his wife's age, you see. Summer solstice, after which the days get shorter. Sun sets earlier, doesn't it?"

Shapiro agreed that after June twenty-first the days get shorter; that the year has passed its zenith.

"Carol's supposed to be twenty. Which is about what Arlene-baby really is."

"And her husband's around forty? I mean this Louis Derwent?"

"Precisely forty. Bret's script makes a point of it. Same birthday, actually. Only, Carol's is really the winter solstice. It plays—well, simpler than I make it sound."

"But the ages of the two are essential to the—the story of the play?"

"Yes. What it's all about, really. The husband—well, trying to keep up with his young wife. Not that forty's all that old, is it?"

Shapiro agreed that forty was not all that old. "Mr. Branson seemed to be all right when you and Miss Arnold left, Mrs. Abel?"

"Exceedingly. He'd just done the 'To be or not to be.' " She looked at Shapiro for a moment with doubt in her eyes. "Hamlet's soliloquy, you know," she said. "Shakespeare."

As he had nodded at Lord's mention of Hamlet, Shapiro nodded again, to show that his ignorance of the theater was not quite complete.

"Mr. Simon asked him to, Lieutenant. I don't know why, exactly. As part of the celebration, maybe. Clive's Hamlet was a hit in London a few years back. Before he went to Hollywood,

32

that was. Anyway, Clive read it—beautifully, I thought—and everybody gathered around and listened. And applauded afterward. Yes, when Arly and I left, Clive was—oh, on top of the world. Also, I suppose, a little spiffed. But weren't we all? Not really. Just a little. It was a celebration, after all."

"Yes, Mrs. Abel. I suppose, before everybody gathered around to listen to Mr. Branson reciting Shakespeare, people had just been sitting around and talking and—"

"Drinking champagne, Lieutenant. Mostly, anyway. Very good champagne. The waiter kept filling glasses. Only we didn't just sit. We moved around, of course, the way people do at parties. Circulated, you know."

"Yes. Carrying your glasses, I suppose."

"I carried mine. If you left your glass on a table, the waiter would fill it up. Some of us did, of course."

"Did Mr. Branson, did you notice?"

She said, *"Oh.* You mean somebody could put cyanide in his glass? Have a chance to?"

"We don't know, Mrs. Abel. Not cyanide, certainly. Probably nothing at all. We're just feeling our way around, you see. Because Mr. Branson's death was so sudden, so unexpected. Sort of thing we have to do, you know. You didn't happen to notice whether Mr. Branson left his glass standing somewhere when you were all, as you say, circulating?"

"No. Why should I?"

"No reason. I just thought you might have."

"I don't watch what people drink. Oh, Clive was drinking whiskey when Ken and I first got there. Bourbon and water, from the color. He usually did. When I'd take him to lunch, it was always bourbon and water. Last night—I think it was bourbon—to start with, anyway. Maybe champagne later. Does it matter?"

"Not at all, Mrs. Abel. Just trying to get the picture. People moving around and talking. Sometimes leaving their glasses where they'd been sitting, sometimes carrying their glasses along when they—well, joined another group."

"Precisely. Just a relaxed sort of party."

"And Mr. Branson was, as you say, on top of the world when you left?"

"Absolutely. People applauded after his reading. Not the sort who applaud unless they mean it. And Clive's—Clive was an actor. They like applause, you know."

"Yes," Shapiro said. "Put anybody on top of the world, I'd think. By the way, Mr. Branson was one of your clients. Does that mean you negotiated his contract for this play? With Mr. Simon, I suppose?"

"Of course. Run of the play. And—well, a very good contract. Mr. Simon was very anxious to get him, naturally. And, of course, so was Bret."

Bret? Oh, yes—Bret Askew, who had written *Summer Solstice.*

"Do you mind telling us what Mr. Branson's salary was, Mrs. Abel?"

"Yes, Lieutenant, I think I do. Unless it's very important to your—investigation. Let's just say substantial and leave it there, shall we? Or, of course, you can ask Mr. Simon. Maybe he'll tell you, if it's important."

Shapiro nodded. "And will Mr. Price get the same salary, Whatever it was? And the same run-of-the-play contract?"

"God, no, Clive was a star. A famous one. Just his name brought them flocking in. Dear Ken is just a rising young actor. He does want run of the play, as you probably gathered, and I'll try and get him that. But not Clive's salary. Not by—well, thousands. Depends on what the critics say. If they decide to come tomorrow night. If Simon decides to reopen tomorrow night. He's probably deciding about that now, at the rehearsal, you know. That's what they called it for."

"Where will they be having this rehearsal, Mrs. Abel?"

"At the theater, of course. But they won't want outsiders."

Shapiro said he saw.

5

The pretty young receptionist was at her desk when they went out through the outer office of Martha Abel Associates. She was on the telephone. She looked up and smiled a conventional smile. It was midafternoon by then; too early for results of the autopsy on the late Clive Branson. Still—

There were two telephone booths on the lobby floor of the modest office building. Shapiro used one of them.

Dr. Nelson was available at the offices of the Medical Examiner, New York County. Yes, the post mortem examination of the cadaver of Branson, Clive, was under way. No results to be released at the moment. But did Lieutenant Shapiro want a guess? He did.

"Could be natural causes," Nelson said. "Like I told you when we picked it up. Cardiac arrest. Or could be—this is just a guess, Lieutenant—overdose of one of the barbiturates. Along with alcohol. Alcohol in the blood, all right. We've got that far. Bad combination, alcohol and barbiturates. Both depressive, you know."

"High alcohol content in the blood, Doctor?"

"Not especially. He wasn't drunk. He'd been drinking."

"We've been told," Shapiro said, "that Branson never took sleeping pills. That he told his dresser that he overreacted to them. What would he have meant by that, would you say?"

"Probably that they knocked him out sooner than they do most people. Or kept him out longer. Hypersensitive, could be. Or, one chance in hundreds, that they stimulated instead of putting to sleep. Does happen with a few—very few. But it does happen. Makes one person in—oh, a few hundreds, climb walls instead of quietly passing out for a few hours. Eight, maybe. Maybe only six or so. Depends on the dosage, of course. Usual therapeutic dose for Nembutal, for instance, is a hundred mgs. Some people do fine with fifty."

"Yes. And the lethal dose, Doctor?"

"Varies a lot. As little as a gram has been fatal. People have recovered after several times that. Depends on a lot of things. Weight, age, general physical condition. Lot of things."

"Including special sensitivity?"

"Certainly. And whether there's alcohol in the bloodstream, as I just told you. Listen, Shapiro, we haven't finished with this one. A couple of hours to go. And when we've got something, it'll go through channels. O.K.?"

"Of course, Doctor. We—just want to get going. If there's someplace to go."

"Well," Dr. Nelson said, "you can call it a suspicious death. Good enough?"

Shapiro said, "Yes, Doctor," and hung up.

"This *Summer Solstice*'s playing at the Rolf Simon Theater," Tony Cook told him when he came out of the booth. "Forty-sixth, east of Broadway. Easy enough walk from here."

"Yes," Shapiro said. "Strike you that Mrs. Abel and this actor, Price, sound pretty chummy, Tony?"

"Because of the 'darlings' and 'sweethearts'? Maybe. But theater people do talk that way quite a lot. Rachel's sort of picking it up since she got those TV jobs."

Rachel Farmer, by profession a model for painters and pho-

37

tographers, had recently got bit parts in several TV series epi-
sodes—parts which required tall girls. She is almost as tall as
Tony Cook, a fact which they often verify.

Shapiro said, "Mmm," and by unspoken agreement they
started walking toward the Rolf Simon Theater. When they had
gone a few blocks, Shapiro said, "Probably just that, I suppose.
Still, she's a handsome woman, Tony. And not married. Not
working at it, anyway. And they did seem rather chummy."

"And Branson's death is a break for Price. Only they're both
her clients, Nate. And Branson was a star, with a star's salary.
Of which La Abel got her cut. A lot bigger cut than she'll get
from Price's. I don't mean a bigger percent; bigger total."

"I know what you mean," Shapiro said, and they waited for a
green light to cross where Broadway and Seventh Avenue meet.

The Rolf Simon Theater was on the south side of Forty-sixth,
in the middle of the block. The sign read:

CLIVE BRANSON
IN
Summer Solstice
a new comedy
by BRET ASKEW

"Branson" was in much larger lettering than "Askew" or, for
that matter, than the title of the play. It was also outlined in
light bulbs, which Askew's was not. The theater lobby was
brightly lighted. Half a dozen people stood in line in front of the
box-office counter. And there was a sign which read, in letters of
still-damp paint:

No Performance Tonight
Refund requests by mail from Rolf Simon Productions

The center door to the auditorium was closed. It was not

locked, as they found while the man in the box office yelled, "Hey!" at them. They paid no attention to the "Hey."

The stage was lighted harshly from above. Three men made up the audience. On stage, Ken Price, facing a very pretty young woman in a green pantsuit, said, "The minute you were born, darling, the days began to get longer. With me, it was the other way around."

The man on the aisle got up from his seat and walked toward the stage and said, "Not like that, for God's sake, Price. The way Clive read it. This is comedy, man. *Comedy.*"

"O.K., O.K.," Price said. "I know it's comedy, Mr. Kirby. I'm trying to read it that way. But is that line supposed to roll them in the aisles?"

"Not the way you're reading it," a slim young man said from his orchestra seat. "And here in the fifth row I can just hear you."

"Sorry," Price said, and read the line again, more loudly and with more vivacity.

"More like it," the man named Kirby said. "A little more like it. So, Miss Collins? Taking a little nap or something?"

"Longer days," the pretty young woman said. "Oh, ever so much longer." But, to Shapiro, there seemed to be almost a sob underlying her voice. Shapiro and Cook sat down in the back row.

"Jesus H. Christ!" Kirby said. "All right, take five and we'll go on with the funeral. Act Two again from the top." He sat again in his aisle seat, next to a heavy-set man with gray hair.

Tony Cook had found a program and was looking at it. "Comedy in three acts by Bret Askew," he read from it, keeping his voice low. "Directed by Robert Kirby."

But his voice had not been low enough. The heavy-set man turned in his seat and looked at them. His broad face was as

39

heavy-set as his body. He stood up and Kirby got out of his seat to let him pass. The man was also tall; coming up the aisle he was formidable. When he was three or four rows away, he spoke. His voice, too, was heavy.

"All right, you two," he said. "What're you doing here? And how the hell did you get in?"

"We're policemen, Mr. Simon," Shapiro said, taking a chance on the identity of the producer. "And nobody tried to stop us. We can just wait until you've finished."

"You've got names, I suppose," Simon said, conceding by absence of contradiction that Shapiro had been right about his own. "And wait for what, man?"

Shapiro gave him names. "To talk about Mr. Branson's death," he added. "His very sudden death. We're from Homicide, Mr. Simon."

"So what the—" Rolf Simon said, and stopped. He turned and spoke down the aisle. "All right, Kirby," he said, his voice loud in the almost empty room. "Get on with it. Have the new boy read . . . you, Peter. You'll have to be up on it by tomorrow, if you want the part."

A somewhat wraithlike young man spoke from the stage, on which he had been relatively invisible. He said, "O.K., Mr. Simon. I'll be up on it by tomorrow."

Simon made, loudly, the sound usually described as "Hmph." Then he said, "All right, you two, we may as well go upstairs."

The "you two" was clearly for Shapiro and Tony Cook. They followed Simon out into the lobby.

Now there were eight men and women in front of the box office. The man inside looked at Rolf Simon and raised his eyebrows. Simon merely shook his head.

Beyond the box office, Simon stopped in front of a narrow

40

door. He used a key to open it. It opened on an elevator, almost as narrow as the door. There was just room for the three of them in it—and that, primarily, because Nathan Shapiro, although a tall man, is a thin one. The elevator went up, for what seemed to Shapiro rather a long time. When it stopped, it was at an office with a young woman in it. She was typing when Simon led them into the office. The young woman looked up with the expression suitable for an expectant secretary.

"Okay, sweetheart, you can take a break," Simon said. "Matter of fact, you can call it a day."

"But Mr. Simon—" she said.

"Tomorrow," Simon said.

She got up and went out through a door at the rear of the office. With the door open, Shapiro could see what looked to be a large living room.

"Yes," Simon said. "Rolf Simon Productions and living quarters." The secretary called Sweetheart closed the door after her.

"Trouble with actors," Simon said, "they get to thinking they're people. Louses things up."

Shapiro could think of no answer to that, and so attempted none.

"Sit down somewhere," Simon said and went himself to a big desk and sat behind it. "Look at that damn girl. All mushed up. Damn near puddling, wasn't she?"

Shapiro said, "Sorry, Mr. Simon."

"Just saw her, if you were looking," Simon said. "Heard her, too. Damn near crying, wasn't she? Poor little wench had a crush on him. Don't call it a crush nowadays, I suppose. A thing for him. God knows what they do call it. Anyway, she's all broken up. Have to snap out of it by tomorrow night. Probably will, I guess. Nice little actress. She got decent notices, anyway."

It seemed to Shapiro that Rolf Simon put a slight emphasis on the word "she." Perhaps, he thought, the emphasis was not intentional.

"You're talking about Miss Collins—I think that's her name, isn't it? And her having this crush, or whatever they call it, on Mr. Branson?"

"What else, Shapiro? Not that it was doing her any good, I'll say that for Branson. Did realize she was years too young for him. Like in the play. Well, almost like in the play, let's say. Jesus, how'd I let Askew talk me into this? Ought to know better at my age, wouldn't you say?"

Shapiro decided he had no answer for that one either.

"And Branson wasn't interested in Miss Collins, Mr. Simon?"

"Said he wasn't, anyway; didn't play around much, far's I know. Not lately, anyhow. Men get past it, Shapiro. Some do, anyway. As you'll learn one of these days."

Shapiro supposed so. He nodded his head in acceptance of the nondurability of the human male.

"Sure," Simon said, "some hold out longer than others. But Clive Branson was—well, sort of a quiet guy. As actors go. A sweet guy, you could say. Everybody liked him. And here you two are saying somebody killed him. What the hell, Lieutenant?"

"We don't say that, Mr. Simon. Only that it's possible. What we call a suspicious death; what the medical examiner calls it. No doctor around. So, no death certificate."

"He was all right last night," Simon said. "Far's I could tell, anyway. Did that Hamlet bit O.K. Fond of doing that, old Clive was. Sort of—well, sort of a set piece, if you know what I mean."

"Yes," Shapiro said. "I understand you arranged this party,

42

Mr. Simon. To celebrate Mr. Branson's birthday. That was yesterday? His birthday, I mean."

"Nearest Sunday to it, anyway. Day we're not on, you know. Night off. Years ago, it was against the law to have performances on Sunday. Isn't anymore, but it's still a day off. For my shows, anyway. Got set in my ways, you could call it."

Shapiro nodded again. At a guess, Rolf Simon had had plenty of time to get set in his ways. Somewhere around seventy years, the guess would be. Which brought the question up again.

"Do you know how old Mr. Branson was, Mr. Simon?"

"Older than he—no, Lieutenant, I don't know how old Branson was. Been around quite a while, I do know. In *Who's Who* it figures out—"

"I know," Shapiro said. "Figures out to be forty-two, but they'd take his word for that, wouldn't they?"

"Far's I know. All right, maybe he was a couple of years older. Didn't show it—not to me, anyway. As I said, he was going great guns last night. Some of these damn squirts ought to have seen him then." He stopped speaking rather abruptly and stared at Shapiro. His stare, like everything else about him, was heavy.

"What squirts, Mr. Simon?"

"All right—these damn reviewers. Call themselves critics. Different breed of cats fifty years ago. Called themselves critics then, too, but some of them were. Nathan. Joe Krutch. Some of the others. Nowadays—" He did not add to that. His inflection made more unnecessary.

"The reviewers didn't give *Summer Solstice* good—write-ups, Mr. Simon?"

"Reviews. Notices." Simon said. "Oh, the *Chronicle* liked the play well enough. Compared it to S. N. Behrman *and* Noel Coward. Takes us back a few years, doesn't it? But it was an all-right notice, and the *Chronicle*'s the one that counts. And the *Sentinel* wasn't bad, except it messes around with the word 'veteran.' 'Far too veteran for the forty-year-old husband.' Or some such, for God's sake."

"Referring to Mr. Branson?"

"Who else? Made him sound doddering, 'miscast by about ten years.' "

"That Branson was too old for the part?"

"I suppose so. Character's supposed to be forty. Wife's twenty. What the play's all about. You can have a look at the show tomorrow night, Lieutenant. If we get the kinks out by then. Leave you a couple of tickets at the box office. For you, too, Cook, if that's your name."

Tony Cook admitted that was his name.

"House seats if it comes to that," Simon said. "Sold out solid until after Christmas, but this may put a dent in it. Hard to tell about that. You know what a summer solstice is, Lieutenant?"

Shapiro did know. "The date the day is at its longest," he said. "Most daylight compared to darkness. June twenty-first most years."

"Yeah. And winter solstice the other way around—December twenty-first or -second. The way Askew's rigged it, the girl—this Mrs. Derwent—was born on December twenty-first, and her husband on June twenty-first. Only he was born twenty years before she was. Twenty years and a half, actually. O.K., it's a gimmick, but it works out, all right. Light comedy; sort of thing we don't get too much of nowadays. The boy can write, I'll give him that. Hell, even these damn reviewers give him that. But it was Branson who brought them in. Made the advance sale. Star-of-stage-and-screen sort of thing. For all he was a nice guy."

"And," Shapiro said, "for all you knew a healthy one?"

"He never said he wasn't. And didn't look as if he wasn't. But I hadn't been seeing him lately. Back in Hollywood, he did tell me once he was having some trouble sleeping, but who doesn't? I told him I wasn't sleeping too damn well, either, except I was taking pills for it. And he said something about envying me, whatever he meant by that."

Shapiro said he saw. He said, "Mr. Branson had a run-of-the-play contract, I gather. Mind telling me what salary you were paying him, Mr. Simon?"

"Yes, I do mind. Gets out and people will think I was a damn fool. Think I'm a soft touch. I was paying him plenty. And, yes, run of the play. That he held out for, and I can't say I blame him."

Shapiro stood up. "So," he said. "I guess we can let Mr. Simon get back to his rehearsal, don't you, Cook?"

By which Tony Cook knew it was his turn. And, for a moment, he was puzzled by what his turn should come to. Then he made a stab at it.

"When did this party last night break up, Mr. Simon?" Cook asked.

"Hell," Simon said, "I didn't keep a stopwatch on it. A little after one, at a guess. Clive began emptying ashtrays. Had a little gadget to put butts in, and began emptying trays into it. Not the sort of thing I'd ever seen him do on the West Coast, but what the hell? His house, after all."

"Probably thought the party was about over," Tony Cook said.

"Or ought to be," Simon agreed. "So—I figured he was bored, or maybe sleepy. Can't say I was myself; ready to make a night of it, actually. So were the others, I thought. Kirby and Bret Askew, anyway. Arlene and Mrs. Abel had split already. The Abel dame suggested that. Business about being a working

45

girl. Having to be at the office first thing in the morning. Lot of crap, of course. Actors' agents open their offices around eleven, which is about the time actors begin to wake up. Anyway, that's what she said. And Arlene decided to go along with her. And Ken Price took off about a quarter of an hour later, which didn't surprise me a hell of a lot."

"No, Mr. Simon?" Shapiro said. "Why?"

"Oh, no special reason."

Shapiro waited, but Rolf Simon did not amplify.

"But you were surprised when Mr. Branson started clearing up—as if the party was over?"

"Well, a little, I guess. Not like old Clive. He always liked parties. Seemed to in Hollywood, anyway. But, as I said, I hadn't seen him for several years. Maybe he'd changed. Wasn't so hot for parties anymore. Look, how do I know? We weren't buddies. He was—well, you can say he was working for me. And I threw the party sort of to keep him happy."

"He wasn't happy, Mr. Simon?"

"I didn't mean that. Actors—well they take a bit of soft-soaping. Stroking of their goddamn egos. Clive less than most, come to that. But he was still an actor. Damn nice guy, but under that an actor. And a star, for God's sake. And after all, it was his house. He could call the turn, if he wanted to. But I had to make the move, of course."

Shapiro said he saw.

"Waited a few minutes after the cleanup act, so as not to make it too obvious, and—well, led the retreat. Clive saw us out and said all the right things and then, I guess, went upstairs to bed. And I came back here and did the same thing."

"Mr. Branson had an appointment to have some sketches made this morning," Shapiro said. "With a Miss Hunt. Part of a layout for the *Chronicle,* I understand. Did you know about that, Mr. Simon?"

"Knew Alex was setting something up like that, yes. Didn't know the details."

"Alex?"

"Alex Bernheim. Does my publicity. Could be, Clive wanted to get a good night's sleep before having his picture taken. Might account for the cleanup act, I suppose."

"Drawn," Shapiro said. "Miss Hunt does sketches. Well—" He moved toward the elevator door.

"I'll go down with you," Simon said. "See how Bob's making out. Whether he's got Arlene to quit crying into her lines."

So the three of them rode down together in the small and evidently very private elevator.

6

In the lobby there was still a short line in front of the box-office window. The people in the line had changed, but their number remained constant. Again the man in the box office raised his eyebrows at Rolf Simon. Then he jerked up his thumb and nodded his head and smiled widely. Whatever the people in the line were there for, the box office man was cheerful about it. Simon nodded at the box-office window and went toward one of the doors opening on the orchestra.

Shapiro and Cook went with him. With the door open, Simon checked and turned to look at Shapiro.

"Yes," Shapiro said, "but we'll try not to take long."

Robert Kirby and Price were now alone on the stage. Kirby was sitting on a sofa, and Price, standing, was looking down at him.

"That's the winter solstice, darling," Kirby said.

"Yes," Price said. "The minute you were born, darling, the—"

"No," Kirby said. "For God's sake no, Ken. Look, you're forty. Forty and six months. Your wife's an even twenty. You're trying to be her age. But not, for Christ's sake, *sixteen*. Here, like this." Kirby stood up and faced Ken Price. " 'The minute you were born, darling, the days started to get longer' . . . Get what I mean?"

"I think so," Price said. He read the line again. There was a difference in the new reading.

"Better," Kirby said. "Soon as Collins comes back, we'll take it from the top. Where the hell's that coffee?"

"Coming right up, Mr. Kirby," a voice said from the wings. "Didn't know you were ready to break." A middle-aged man followed his voice from the wings. He had a mug in each hand and gave them to Kirby and Ken Price.

Kirby said, "Thanks, Harry." He carried his cup down from the stage, crossing a short, obviously temporary gangway and descending an equally improvised flight of steps. He started toward a seat beside the slight young man who had been there before, but he stopped when he saw Rolf Simon lumbering down the aisle.

Simon said, "Well?"

"Shaping up," Kirby said. "Ken's getting it. The girls's still blubbering. Little Miss Broken-heart. I gave her a break. She went to her dressing room, I guess. Time to dry out. But the kid's a trooper. She'll come out of it."

"By tomorrow night?" Simon said.

"We can hope. But yes, R.S., I think so."

The slight man got up from his seat and joined Robert Kirby, also facing Simon. "Arly will be all right, Mr. Simon," he said. "A little in shock, and why not? Aren't we all?"

"To a degree, Mr. Askew," Simon said, "I suppose we are. But we don't have to start playing opposite a different man, do we?" Simon turned to Nathan Shapiro. "This is Bret Askew, Lieutenant. Man who wrote the play. Helped get Branson interested in the part."

"Clive Branson was a great actor," Askew said. "But Price is getting it. Lieutenant?"

Askew was a slim, rather handsome man, probably in his early thirties or late twenties; a man who, from the inflection of his voice, did not think Nathan Shapiro looked particularly like a lieutenant. Shapiro doesn't, either. He explained what kind of

49

lieutenant he was. Askew said, "Oh," but not as if much had been explained.

"In connection with Branson's death," Simon said, "Seems they're going to raise some question about it. They're asking about last night's party. What Lieutenant Shapiro is here for. And Detective Cook."

Askew said, "Oh," again. Then he said, "What the hell? They think one of us did Clive in?"

Shapiro answered that. "We don't know that anybody did Mr. Branson in, Mr. Askew. We're merely trying to make sure that somebody didn't. Very sudden, the death seems to have been. We don't like sudden unexplained deaths, you see."

"Who does, Lieutenant? But who would want to kill old Clive? Swell guy and one hell of an actor. Price, there, is all right. Maybe a bit more than all right. But it was Clive Branson who had us going. Had my play going, is what I mean. Got what I was driving at. Not that Bob here doesn't. And Mr. Simon of course. But there's only so much a director can do, come down to it. Depends on the people he's got to work with, doesn't it?"

Shapiro supposed it did, and said so. He also said it was not his line of country. He merely thought, but did not say, that Askew was talking a good deal, and rather nervously. Under a strain, presumably. His first Broadway play, Martha Abel had said, and a success; might run for years. And the actor who "had my play going" had ceased, overnight, to have anything going at all. Reason enough to be nervous; to be, like Arlene Collins, in shock.

"You thought Mr. Branson was feeling all right last night, Mr. Askew? Not depressed, or anything like that?"

"Never saw him better," Askew said. "That's right, isn't it, Mr. Simon? Kirby?"

"Top form, I thought," Robert Kirby said, and finished his

50

coffee. "Well, we may as well get on with it. With or without our pretty little crybaby. Only—well, eventually we've got to work them in together, don't we? Ken can go on bouncing lines off me, but it will need more than that. And I told her to take a few minutes' break. Not a few hours."

He turned and went back down the aisle, carrying his empty mug. He climbed to the stage, where Price had sat on the sofa and was finishing his coffee. He got up as Kirby came onto the stage.

The sofa was one of several pieces of furniture in a living room where, upstage, the wall was sliding glass doors, through which the audience could see a terrace with bright-colored outdoor furniture on it.

On the stage, Kirby said, "Harry!" his voice pitched high.

Harry came out of the wings and took the coffee mugs from the two men.

"And Harry," Kirby said, "have them light the set, huh? May as well see what we're doing."

Harry said, "O.K.," and started back toward the door he had come through, downstage left.

"And Harry, you might drop by Miss Collins's room and ask her if she's up to going on with it."

Harry said, "O.K."

But Askew said, "Better let me do that, hadn't you, Bob?"

"If you want to," Kirby said, without turning to face the playwright. "O.K., Price. . . . 'That's the winter solstice, darling.'"

"The minute you were born, darling, the days started to get longer. And the sun got higher."

"Okay, Ken. You're getting it. A little more upbeat on that sun bit. All right?"

Price read the line again, presumably with more upbeat. Askew went down the aisle and climbed to the stage. Simon said, "Well, gentlemen?"

51

"All for right now, I guess," Shapiro said. "Could be we'll be back."

"Depending, I suppose, on what turns up in the autopsy, Lieutenant?"

Shapiro said, "Yes, among other things. Tony?"

Tony Cook and Shapiro went out toward the lobby. As Tony was closing the door behind them, the light changed. They looked back. The terrace of the set now was flooded with what appeared to be sunlight. The light poured through the glass wall of the living room. "Nice setup the Derwents have," Tony said. "Very upper class, looks like they are. Does it occur to you, Nate, that we haven't had lunch?"

"Yes. Also that we'd better check in."

There was a bar and grill across the street. They agreed it looked passable, or near enough, and crossed the street. Just inside, there was a telephone booth. Shapiro went into it. Tony went to the bar. A fat barman was the only occupant of the restaurant. It was, after all, between three and four in the afternoon, and a lull was to be expected.

The barman was taking advantage of it in a chair behind the bar. He said "Help you?" to Tony, without sounding much as if he wanted to, and without getting up from the chair. No, they didn't have draft beer. Yes, they did have Bud. Sure, it was cold. He stood up then and got two bottles of Budweiser from an ice bin under the bar. He slid the bottles to Tony Cook, who slid money back to him. The barman sat down again.

All right, Chet could rustle up food for them, probably, although the kitchen was supposed to be closed. "Just ring from one of the booths."

Tony carried the cold bottles to the nearest booth. He found the button which presumably would ring Chet's bell. He did not press it, waiting for Nathan Shapiro.

Detective (2nd. gr.) Thompson was catching in the squad room at Manhattan South. Yes, Captain—sorry, Inspector— Weigand had come in about half an hour ago. But at the moment he was on the telephone. "Sure, Lieutenant, I'll put you on hold."

Shapiro stayed on hold for several minutes. Then Bill Weigand said, "O.K., Nate. Dorian seems to have got you into something."

"Could be," Nathan said. "I don't really know yet, Inspector. Congratulations, Inspector."

He was told to come off it.

Shapiro said, "All right. But you had it coming, Bill."

Weigand said "Mmm," and, "Had the M.E.'s office on the phone. A Dr. Nelson. Seems they've pretty much finished on Branson. Found a barbiturate. But not much of it. Probably ingested about a gram. More than the therapeutic dose, but not likely to be lethal. Alcohol in the blood, too, but not too much of that, either. Thing seems to be, the average person could just as well be alive. Nelson said they'd have been quite puzzled by it, but he'd heard the report from you that the deceased had a history of overreaction to barbiturates."

"Yes," Shapiro said. "His dresser—valet, whatever—said Branson had told him he'd found that out years ago. Couldn't tolerate any sleeping pills."

"And may have told other people, Nate?"

"Could be. We'll have to ask around. By the way, did the pathologist make a guess as to Branson's age?"

"Middle to late fifties, possibly sixty. But, as they say, well preserved. Does it enter in?"

"I don't know. On the chance it does, maybe, I'm asking around."

"O.K.—because it's our baby now. Precinct's passed it along

53

to squad. Formal referral. Cook's with you, I suppose? Not around here, anyway."

"Tony's with me. Sitting in a booth in this restaurant. We didn't get around to lunch until just now."

"Late for it. Dorian will be pleased, by the way—not that maybe somebody killed Branson, of course, but that she didn't set us to barking up a wrong tree. I mean one with no coon in it. By the way, Nate, I'm recommending that you take over here, when they decide where to put me. Will probably go through. And you'll make acting captain if it does. At least acting."

Shapiro could think of only one response to that. It was, *"Jesus."* He made it.

"I know, Nate," Bill Weigand said. "You think the department's gone off its rocker."

Since Nathan Shapiro believes the New York Police Department has been off its rocker since it approved his entirely experimental application for promotion to lieutenant, he said merely, "Be checking in, Inspector," and went off to join Cook in the booth.

He approved the beer, since Tony had already bought it. They poured. Tony pressed the button which was supposed to ring for somebody called Chet. Chet apparently was also enjoying the lull, but in five minutes he showed up. He was as fat as the barman and wore a not especially clean white apron. He said, "Yeah?" and then that the kitchen was closed until six and he didn't know. Nothing hot, that was for sure. Maybe a cold roast beef sandwich. All right, maybe two cold roast beef sandwiches. All right, he'd try to see that one of them was rare. He did not seem optimistic, and Tony Cook was not either.

They had finished their beers and Tony was gesturing the barman, Who was resolutely not looking, when two customers came in. One was Bret Askew, author of *Summer Solstice*. The other was the very pretty young woman in a green pantsuit. As they came in, Askew took his arm from around Arlene Collins's waist.

Perhaps the rehearsal across the street was over. Perhaps Miss Collins had merely not rejoined it.

The barman stood up for them. Askew said, "Hi, Joe. Couple of coffees. And Miss Collins could do with a dry sherry. Very dry. Tio Pepe, if you've got one chilled."

The barman said, "Sir."

The arrival of the two apparently familiar customers appeared to animate the barman. He reached under the bar and, to judge from his movement, pressed something. Chet's summoning bell? Evidently, since it brought Chet. It did not bring cold roast beef sandwiches.

Chet said, "Afternoon, Miss Collins, Mr. Askew. Get you something?"

Askew said, "Coffee, Chet."

"Coming right up, Mr. Askew."

It was suddenly chummy in the bar and grill. Well, the restaurant was across the street from the Rolf Simon Theater. Convenient. Of course, Harry provided coffee to the theater's stage. Perhaps the bar and grill provided better coffee. Possibly, it also provided escape and a measure of privacy. And Arlene Collins seemed to have cheered up; at least she was no longer crying.

Askew picked up the bottle and the glass the barman slid to him. He held them both in one hand and touched the girl's arm with the fingers of the other. He said, "O.K., baby." They walked down the long, thin barroom to a booth at the end of it. They did not appear to see Shapiro and Cook in the booth they walked past. Askew kept his hand on the girl's arm and looked down at her. She showed no indication of a desire to get away.

"Well," Tony said, keeping his voice down. "Looks as if she's

55

coming out of shock, wouldn't you say? Off with the old, on with the new."

"Not all that new, at a guess, Tony," Shapiro said, his own voice not much above a whisper. "But it doesn't need to mean anything."

Tony Cook nodded in agreement. He did say, "Still," dragging it out a little.

Chet reappeared, this time with a tray. The tray had two cups on it and a glass coffee jug. He served the two in the distant booth and went away again. Tony went to the bar and got two more bottles of Budweiser. They were well into them when Chet brought two sandwiches, both of roast beef, but neither of them rare. Neither of them was even pink.

They ate the sandwiches. Tony tried catsup on his, which didn't help much. This time it was Nathan who said, "Well." Then he nodded his head at Tony Cook, who got out of the booth and went to the bar. Joe had sat down again. Tony slid a twenty-dollar bill across the bar. He didn't have anything smaller. The barman stood up, not very rapidly. He turned to the cash register behind the bar.

"Not very busy today, are you?" Tony said.

"Never are in the afternoon. Except Wednesdays—a few come in then. At intermissions, I guess. After the show, a few. But they're mostly women go to matinees, you know. Evenings are our time, when there's a show running across the street. Pretty busy then, some nights. Murph puts two barmen on then. Here's your change."

He spread change on the bar in front of Tony. Tony let a dollar of it stay there. The barman looked at it and then at Tony, who nodded. The barman said, "Thanks, Mac," And picked up the dollar bill.

"Nice-looking girl just came in," Tony said. "Come in often,

56

Joe? Got a feeling I've seen her before somewhere."

"Actress," Joe said, "in that show across the street. No, I wouldn't say often. Now and then, last few weeks. Few weeks back, when they were still rehearsing or something, I guess it was, used to come in for a sherry sometimes."

He went back to his chair.

"Alone?" Tony said.

"Can't say I remember she did. With an older man a few times. And once anyway with an older dame. A couple of times with Mr. Askew, like today. My hunch is, you won't make any time with her, Mac, if that's what you've got in mind."

"Be worth trying," Tony said. "Miss Collins, you called her?"

"Yeah. In that play across the street. *Summer* something, they call it. *Summer Success?* Something like that anyway. Buy a ticket and you can go look at her, Mac."

Tony said, "Yeah. You say she used to come in here with an older man. Remember his name, Joe?"

"No. Never heard it. Say, what are you, Mac? Cop or something?"

"Or something," Tony said. "Just interested in a pretty girl. As who isn't, pal?"

"Me," Joe said. "Oh, there was a time I was. Not much, nowadays, you could say. Leave that to the youngsters, like you, Mac."

Tony said, "Thanks, Joe," and joined Shapiro.

"Used to come in with an older man," he told Shapiro. "Not so often with Askew. With this older man when, he thinks, they were rehearsing what he thinks is called *Summer Success*. And they're busy here in the evenings. During intermissions."

"Figures," Shapiro said. "Guess we'll be going around to see Mrs. Abel for a few minutes, Tony. I gave her a ring, so she'll be expecting us this time. She can't imagine what more she can tell us, and did someone really kill dear Clive? I told her we think somebody did. With a barbiturate, according to the autopsy."

"In an amount which probably wouldn't have killed most people," Tony said.

"Yes, but I didn't tell her that."

"Because maybe she knows, Nate?"

"Well," Shapiro said, "looks as if somebody did, wouldn't you say?"

7

The pretty young receptionist lifted the telephone on her desk when she saw Shapiro and Cook come into the outer office of Martha Abel Associates. She pressed a button in the phone's base and spoke into the phone. They were at her desk by then and could hear her say, "Those policemen are here, Mrs. Abel." There was a rustling sound from the receiver, and the receptionist said, "Yes, Mrs. Abel." She looked up at Shapiro then and said, "You can go right in."

Shapiro rapped on the door to the inner office and Martha Abel said, "Oh, come on in," as if she had been waiting a long time for them. To Shapiro she looked alert, almost to the point of impatience. She raised groomed eyebrows toward him. Then she said, "Well, you're back. I suppose that means"—she paused—"something," she said.

"Autopsy report," Shapiro said, "Preliminary, anyway. Thought you'd want to know."

"Yes?"

"Apparently," Shapiro said, "Mr. Branson took an overdose of one of the barbiturates. Easy to do when you've been drinking. And a bad idea when you've been drinking. You say he seemed in good spirits at the party. Not depressed or anything."

"I told you that. Are you trying to suggest Clive took this overdose you call it on purpose? To kill himself? You couldn't be

59

more wrong, Lieutenant. What reason would he have had? Anyway . . ." She left the "anyway" hanging.

"No, Mrs. Abel. I'm not suggesting anything. Anyway what?"

"Nothing. I don't know what I was going to say."

"Perhaps that Mr. Branson never took sleeping medicine? Not barbiturates, anyway? And so wouldn't have had them around to take?"

"Who told you that? That Clive had low tolerance for barbiturates? Almost no tolerance at all, from what he said."

"His dresser, Mrs. Abel. Man named Lord."

"Poor dear Edgar. Devoted to Clive. Hard to imagine what he'll do now, after so many years. He told you about Clive and sleeping pills?"

"Yes, and I take it he'd know after, as you say, so many years. How did *you* know, Mrs. Abel?"

"Clive told me. Oh, just in passing. I'd said something about having trouble sleeping. It was just after"—she paused—"well, it was just after my husband took off. I was a little upset for a while. Had trouble sleeping. I happened to mention it to Clive, who'd rallied around like the sweet man he is—I mean was, don't I? I told him I was taking sleeping pills and that they seemed to be working. Capsules, actually. Nembutal. Prescription. And he said I was lucky to be able to and that he envied me. Because he couldn't. Was—oh, allergic to them or something. He said, 'What gives most people a few hours of sleep puts me out for weeks—could be even for good,' and that he'd fortunately learned that the first time he ever took a barbiturate."

"Do you know whether he told other people that, Mrs. Abel? About this overreaction?"

She had no idea. She supposed he might have, although he wasn't one of those who went around talking about their health.

"Nembutal," Shapiro said, his tone thoughtful, as if the word had prompted memories. "What my wife took a while back. When she was going up for her oral and—well, found it a little difficult to sleep."

"Oral?"

"Oh, you know—quiz by learned professors for her doctorate. She's a schoolteacher, Mrs. Abel. Principal, now. Since she's *Doctor* Shapiro. Took the stuff for two or three weeks along then. A hundred mgs at bedtime. 'As needed for sleep,' the prescription read. Yes, that was it, a hundred mgs. Sound right to you?"

"Comes in capsules," she said. "Fifties and one-hundreds, I think. Mine were the hundreds. I didn't use up the bottle. Probably kicking around somewhere. Bottle had one of those child-proof caps. Damn near me-proof too, come to that."

"Yes," Shapiro said, "the way my wife's came. I had to help her get the cap off. Hers are probably kicking around somewhere, too. Mg—milligram—that's a thousandth of a gram, isn't it? So ten capsules would add up to a gram."

"And a gram has been known to be fatal," Martha Abel said. "Even to people with normal tolerance. And it would be easy to cut a capsule open. Cut ten capsules open, and put the powder in—oh, in a twist of paper. Ready to spill into somebody's drink. Only—I didn't, Lieutenant. So you didn't need to use this story about this mythical wife of yours."

"All right," Shapiro said. "Only my wife isn't mythical. Dr. Rose Shapiro, principal of Clayton High School, down in the Village."

"So," she said. "I had means and opportunity. That's the way it's phrased, isn't it? But not sole opportunity, you'll have to admit. And how about motive, Lieutenant? Clive Branson had been a friend of mine for years. He was also a client—a very valuable client. Worth—oh, thousands a year in commissions—while he was alive. Dead, worth nothing. Just a longtime friend gone. Don't you have to warn me, or something, Lieutenant Shapiro?"

"Only if I charge you with something. Which I'm not doing, you see. I suppose you don't know who else at this party last night might be taking barbiturates?"

"I've no idea. Any of them might be. Theater people—well, they can be a nervy lot. It's a trying trade, Lieutenant. Or profession. Actors like to call it an art. They—"

The telephone on her desk interrupted her. She said, "Yes?" and then, "Well, if he is, you can't stop him, can you?" And then the door of her office opened with something like violence, and Kenneth Price came in and said *"Darling!"* and, seeing Cook and Shapiro in the room, stopped with that.

"Yes, dear," Martha Abel said. "Gracie could have told you I wasn't free. If you'd given her a chance, that is."

"All right, sweetheart, sorry. Entertaining the police again? They do get around, don't they? If they're all that important to us, O.K. Anyway, I've talked to the grand mogul and—well, well, *we're in.* I thought you might like to know."

"You talked to Mr. Simon?"

"What I just said, dear. I go on tomorrow night. Oh, another run-through tonight. With Arlene. But Kirby seems to be satisfied. Says I'm 'shaping up.' Simon passed that along. Said you can get in touch with him anytime about a new contract."

"Good. I'll do that, Ken. You didn't—anyway, I hope you didn't—try to set anything up yourself? Like run of the play?"

"You ought to know better, lover. Like they say about lawyers. Same with agents. I do know that."

"Yes. It is pretty much the same. 'A fool for a client.' Which did originate with lawyers, of course. So run along, sonny."

Kenneth Price said, "O.K., Marty. We ought to break maybe around ten. After that be all right?"

"Call me when you break. But so far as I know, yes. Although you ought to be getting up on the part."

"I am now. Told you that, didn't I?"

She said, "All right. Give me a ring. And we'll talk about what to hold out for with Simon."

Price said, "See you, dear," and went out of the office.

Shapiro stood up. He said, "Maybe we've bothered Mrs. Abel enough for now, Tony. And—thank you, Mrs. Abel."

"I'm not under arrest?" The pretty white-haired woman smiled when she said it. Shapiro shook his head. He did smile back at her.

Outside the offices of Martha Abel Associates, in the elevator going down, Shapiro said, "Well, Tony? More than agent-client relationship? Or just the way theater people talk? All the 'darlings' and 'sweethearts'?

"And," Tony said, "apparently they have a date for tonight. At her place, at a guess."

"My guess too," Shapiro said. "Not entirely a business date, I'd think. She's an attractive woman, Tony, white hair or not. Although it does make her look older than she is, of course."

"My mother," Tony Cook said, "had completely white hair when she was twenty-five or thereabouts. What my father told me, anyway. But she's got a point about no motive, Nate. Get her boyfriend a better part, sure—but lose a better client. She's a businesswoman, Nate. In what I'd guess is a pretty competitive business. Thousands well lost for love?"

Shapiro said he didn't know; that it was one of the things they'd have to try to find out. Then he said, "Actors have some sort of union, don't they?"

"Actors Equity," Shapiro repeated. "And didn't you tell me a

63

while back that your Rachel has joined it?"

"Had to, Nate. Cost her a bit, she says. But somebody'd of-fered her a part. She's always wanted to be an actor, but she's too tall for it—or thought she was. Apparently there are parts for tall girls nowadays. She says it's because everybody's getting taller. I wouldn't know."

"Go up to the Metropolitan sometime, Tony. They've got some suits of armor there, suits knights wore. Very short knights—under the department's minimum. Do you suppose this Equity recommends agents to its members?"

Tony Cook didn't know. He rather doubted it. He said, "You want Rachel to—"

"It might help, if she doesn't mind."

Shapiro looked at his watch. It was well after four o'clock—after the end of their tour of duty. Not that duty ended on any hour.

"Tell you what," he said, "why don't you go down and ask her? If you think she'll be home. Anything she can pick up about Martha Abel Associates. Its—oh, standing in the community, as they say. How lucrative it is. Anything other actors can guess about. Could be Miss Rachel Farmer is looking for an agent herself, couldn't it?"

Tony said that that would be O.K., would be fine. But he couldn't be sure Rachel would be in her apartment on Gay Street, the apartment directly below Tony's own. He had a feel-ing she was posing for a painter. Still—well, the light would be paling out, maybe. Of course, he could try to get her on the phone.

"Better if you see her," Shapiro said. "Use your power of per-suasion. Maybe she won't want to be a cop. And then call it a day, Tony. I'll check you out."

64

Tony said, "Sir," in his most official tone. He added, "And you, Nate?" Which rather diminished formality.

"Home to Brooklyn," Nathan Shapiro said. "Oh, check in first, of course. I may stop by the library. Have a look at back issues of the *Chronicle*. And the *Sentinel* too."

"At the theater pages?"

"At the theater pages. Get along, Tony. And if your Rachel comes up with anything, try me at the squad. If it's anything hot, pass it along to the cap—no, to the inspector. Have to get used to that, won't we?"

"Will Deputy Inspector Weigand be transferred, Nate?"

"Probably. He expects it."

"Too damn bad," Tony said.

They walked to Sixth Avenue, and Tony went into the nearest entrance to the Sixth Avenue subway, on the downtown side. He did not have to wait long for a local, which was not inordinately crowded. It was only a few minutes to the West Fourth Street station, which is the nearest to Gay Street.

* * * * *

Shapiro walked to Fifth Avenue and down it to Forty-second Street. They had washed the library lions, which Shapiro thought rather a pity. He did not go between the now-pallid lions, but used the Forty-second Street entrance. In the newspaper room, papers from a good many American cities were spread out on high, sloping counters. He found the spread of the New York *Chronicle* for September 11. He found the theater page and "The New Play" by Thorsten McClay. He read:

"Summer Solstice," a comedy by Bret Askew which opened last night at the Rolf Simon Theater, is frisky and witty and recalls, without in any sense imitating, the comedies some decades ago of S. N.

65

Behrman. And some may be reminded of Noel Coward at his most lighthearted. It also is a vehicle for the return to Broadway of Clive Branson, after some years of exile in Hollywood.

It should be a cause for rejoicing. That this is only partly so is, I'm afraid, because Mr. Branson, for all his competence, is still too heavy for the vehicle Rolf Simon has selected for his return. If the vehicle does not collapse under his weight, it does seem to me to stagger somewhat.

The play has to do with a well-off Long Island couple whose chief problem is the disparity of age. Carol Derwent is twenty. Her husband, Louis, is twice her age—twice and six months. We meet them on Louis's birthday, which, by one of those coincidences of which playwrights are fond, occurs on June twenty-first. Hence, of course, the title of the play.

Carol, deftly played by Arlene Collins, a very charming young actress almost as new to Broadway as is Mr. Askew, whose first Broadway production this is, was born on December twenty-first, twenty years earlier—twenty years and six months, to be exact, as Mr. Askew carefully is.

From the day she was born, as the author points out, the days began to grow longer; from that of his advent, the days in an idiom of my ancestors, began to "draw in." Both the protagonists are witty about this, Louis somewhat ruefully so.

Two of the characters present in the Long Island manor provide the perhaps obvious plot—Carol's mother, who is only a few years older than her son-in-law, and a man in his twenties, Ronald Foster, who offers triangular complications. If indeed obvious, the play remains gay and lighthearted. A problem racehorse adds to the fun.

Nevertheless, to put it bluntly, Mr. Branson is slightly miscast, which Mr. Simon, usually astute in such matters, should have noticed. Mr. Branson will undoubtedly prove a drawing card. His reputation, so well earned over the years, will attract many to "Summer Solstice."

66

But "over the years" is, I'm afraid, the crux of the matter. Mr. Branson could be more appropriately cast as Miss Collins's father. It all seems rather a pity.

Kenneth Price is at least adequate in the somewhat minor part of Ronald Foster and Helen Barnes is excellent as Carol's haughty and rather bewildered mother.

The play opens—

Shapiro stopped reading as McClay approached a summary of the plot.

Not, certainly, a rave. Except, perhaps, the playwright's contribution.

The *Sentinel* was occupied by a man who, apparently, was checking up on the stock market. The *Sentinel* was the other paper that mattered to the fate of a Broadway play. Among the magazines, *Manhattan* also mattered, if to a lesser degree. But *Manhattan* would be in the periodical room downstairs. Shapiro waited for the stock investor, who didn't look much like one, to finish catching up on the prices. He was writing numbers down in pencil on a pad. He was taking his time about it. He did not look particularly happy.

Finally, he finished. Shapiro took his place and turned to the September 11 issue and to its theater page. The *Sentinel*'s reviewer, who turned out to be a woman, was not one to mince words. The headline above her review read: MISCASTING MARS NEW COMEDY. Under it, *By Phyllis Drummond*:

The Broadway debut of Bret Askew, the author of two pleasant off-Broadway comedies, must be written off as a disappointment. Not that "Summer Solstice," which opened last night at the Rolf Simon, is less witty and amusing than Mr. Askew's earlier plays. As far as one can tell from last night's production, it is basically as sharp and diverting as its predecessors. Now and then the writing glints through the generally laborious performance. But it is only now and then.

Mr. Simon, the producer, has cast the veteran star Clive Branson in the pivotal role of the mature husband of a bright young wife, pleasantly played by a newcomer named Arlene Collins, an extremely pretty young woman and a fairly adept actress—perhaps, under circumstances more fortunate than those in which she finds herself on the Rolf Simon stage, an actress of marked promise. But Branson's labored acting infects Miss Collins's, as it infects the play.

I have termed Branson a veteran and indeed he is—far too veteran for the part of a man of forty, his role in "Summer Solstice." Branson was no tyro when, years ago, he played Hamlet to the esteem of London critics. How many years ago? It would be unkind to remember, or even to speculate. Since those days, he has usually acted in motion pictures, and mostly in comedy roles. And with considerable success.

It is as a movie star that Mr. Simon has returned him to the legitimate stage. And, to put it abruptly, he is some years too old for the role of Louis Derwent in "Summer Solstice." Unfortunately, the author is very precise about the ages of his protagonists. The slight plot turns on these ages. And Mr. Branson is miscast—miscast by ten years, at the very least.

The action, which is primarily reaction, concerns the age-mismated Derwents, Carol Derwent's mother, and another house guest, one Ronald Foster, who is much closer to Carol Derwent's age and aspires to closeness in other aspects. So, the familiar triangle, complicated by a mother who appears to be about the age of her son-in-law. It is one of the problems of the casting that she actually appears several years younger. The triangle thus becomes a quadrangle, and the interplay is wittily exploited in the text of the play, however much it is fumbled on the stage of the Rolf Simon.

We meet the characters on a sunny afternoon in June—the twenty-first of June and birthday of the host. It is an "Anybody for tennis" afternoon, and Askew actually uses that famously antique line, in a wry fashion; it is spoken by Louis Derwent and is intended as a comment on his own maturity. We find the characters at cocktails on the terrace of the Derwents' Long Island House. . . .

Shapiro did not finish that review, either. They obviously were not raves—not likely to bring ticket brokers racing to the box office waving checks, or to form long lines of customers at the box-office windows, unless to cancel and get their money back. If the wire-service reviewers reacted similarly, visitors to the city might also stay away. Of course, the sharpest criticism was of Branson, and there wasn't any more Branson. It wasn't Nathan's worry. After all, if he accepted Simon's invitation, as he probably would, he would be seeing *Summer Solstice* the next night. With Rose in the next seat; with Kenneth Price playing the part of Louis Derwent.

Shapiro went downtown by subway to the second-floor offices of Homicide, Manhattan South. Deputy Inspector William Weigand was gone for the day. Acting Captain Carmichael was in charge of the four-to-midnight shift. The full autopsy report on Clive Branson hadn't come through yet.

Shapiro went home to Brooklyn and to his wife.

8

Rachel Farmer did not answer her doorbell when Tony Cook rang it in the Gay Street entrance. Tony was not greatly surprised. Probably there was still enough north light to paint by and Rachel was still standing, naked and perhaps shivering slightly, in a drafty studio. It is her view that studios are built to accumulate drafts.

Tony rang a second time before he used his key. He would leave a note asking her to come upstairs, or to telephone upstairs, because there was a favor he wanted to ask of her.

But in the living room of the apartment, which overlooks Gay Street, he could hear the shower running in the bathroom off the bedroom. Looking in, he could see Rachel's clothes lying on the bed—the wide bed which had replaced the narrow one she had had there when they met.

He sat down where he could look into the familiar bedroom and waited. He did not have to wait long. The bathroom door opened and Rachel, all the long grace of her, came out into the bedroom. She was not wearing anything. It was warm in the apartment. She saw Tony and said, "Hi." Then, as she walked toward him, she said, "You're early, Tony. Way early. What time is it?"

It was a few minutes after five, and he told her so.

"We said seven," she told him. "Almost two hours early. Not

70

that I mind, although I'd thought of having a nap. But a drink will do as well, I guess." She came out into the living room and sat on the deep sofa. She was still naked, but it was still warm in the apartment. As far as Rachel is concerned clothing is to keep off cold. Oh, and to dress up to go out. Tony got chilled bottles from the refrigerator—dry sherry for Rachel, gin and dry vermouth for himself. He poured her sherry into a chilled glass, mixed his martini, served them both.

He managed not to touch her, although the avoidance was difficult. He did sit on the sofa beside her.

"The thing is," he said, "Nate and I could use your help on something."

"So Branson was murdered," she said. "The radio was pretty vague about it. Sort of evasive. The way it can be, you know."

"Yes, it looks as if he may have been."

"Atwitz keeps the radio on while he's painting. On loud. But he does keep his place reasonably warm, I'll say that for him. I suppose it's warmer if you're wearing something. Help on what, dear?"

"Have you got an agent? I mean one to get you parts in plays."

"No. Only Ray Lambert. You've met him."

Tony had met Ray Lambert, who was an agent for models, not for actors. But Rachel had only in the last year or so been getting acting jobs.

"And," Rachel said, "I'd better get one or give the whole thing up. I can't go on sitting around in casting offices, trying not to look too tall. So what, Tony?"

"You are a member of Actors Equity?"

"Of course. Have to be, if you're a pro. And I'm getting to be a pro, Tony."

He knew she was. He had seen her in a play. Hers was a

71

small part; from Tony's point of view, she stole the show.

He told her he knew she was. He said, "This Equity. Do you suppose it has a list of actors' agents? Of people it can recommend to members?"

She didn't know. Probably it had. But to recommend one over others, she doubted. "Why, Tony?"

He told her why—background and general standing of an agency named Martha Abel Associates.

"I think I've heard of it, dear. But—wait a minute. I know somebody who knows everything about everybody. In the theater, I mean. A very good actress. Always working. And I know where she'll be at—what time is it now? I'm not wearing my watch."

Tony had noticed that, and that she was not wearing anything else, a condition of which she was probably unaware. It was twenty minutes of six.

"Then in about an hour, Janice will be having a drink in the Algonquin lounge. When she's working, which is almost always, she has one drink at six thirty and a bite to eat—just a bite, she says, before the performance. If we hurry, we can catch her in the lounge. Or in the restaurant. If we leave right now and are lucky about a taxi."

She moved on the sofa as if to get up and start looking for a cab.

"Clothes, dear," Tony said. "And I could do with a shower. And a clean shirt."

"You know where the shower is," she told him. "I don't run to clean shirts. That one looks reasonably—"

"Ten minutes," Tony said. "Back by the time you dress."

Upstairs in his own apartment, it took fifteen minutes for him to shower and get into a suit recently back from the cleaners.

Rachel was dressed and ready when he went down. On Sixth Avenue they were lucky with a cab. It was six twenty when they found a place in the Algonquin's lounge-lobby, from which they could see the elevators.

Janice—Janice Towne, it turned out to be—came out of the elevator at precisely six thirty. She was a slim woman, probably in her mid-forties, and wore a gray dress with red splashings which did little to blur the outlines of an admirable body. Rachel started to get up, presumably to wave greeting and invitation to Janice Towne, but Tony touched her arm and shook his head.

"No reason to have to explain me," he told her. "For the moment, we're not together. I'm"—he looked around the room, which was filling, in which bells were tinkling—"over there." He went over there. He watched Rachel, full of innocent surprise and pleasure, summon Janice Towne to the seat he had just vacated. He watched as their table bell brought a waiter hurrying to them. He already had a martini on a tray and put it on the table in front of Miss Towne, who clearly was a patron whose wishes were known and were to be anticipated. Miss Towne evidently said, "Thank you", and the waiter bowed over her drink. He bowed again as he took Rachel's order, of course for a very dry sherry, Tio Pepe if available. Janice Towne began to sip, and the two began to talk.

Tony tapped the bell of his own table. The response was not so prompt. The lounge was filling rapidly. But a waiter did come and take an order for a very dry martini. Tony lighted a cigarette and waited. After a few minutes, his drink came and Janice Towne finished hers and smiled at Rachel and stood up. She went to the restaurant, where the maître d' waited to greet her.

Tony, after a pause, went to join Rachel, carrying his drink.

73

Rachel said, "Is there a *the* Jason Abel you know of, Tony?"

For a moment, Tony could not think of any Jason Abel who merited a *the*. Unless—

"A financier," he said. "One of the country's big fortunes. Maybe the world's big fortunes."

"Sounds right. Mrs. Abel was married to him. For about five years, Janice thinks. Married her when she was a young actress and, as Janice says, very fetching. They split up five or six years ago, Mr. Abel being the major splitter, she thinks. Found somebody even more fetching, the rumor was. Married her, too. Marrying type, apparently. Paid Martha for not making a fuss about it. Rumored amount of settlement, something over a million. So Martha went into the agenting business with a good cushion to lean against. She takes on only top clients: the big names, who get the big salaries and, sometimes, percentages of the gross. Here and in Hollywood."

"Like the late Clive Branson, I gather?"

"Yes, Tony. And even bigger ones. There's no use my trying to get Martha Abel Associates to take me on. Janice did give me the name of a man who might. She's really a sweet person, Janice is."

"Was she curious that you'd be asking about Martha Abel Associates right after Branson's death?"

"She didn't seem to be. I just said I was looking for an agent and had heard of the Abel outfit and what did she think? And wasn't it lucky running into her?"

He told her that it was good going and tapped the bell for another round. They sipped drinks and watched people, a few of whom went directly into the restaurant.

They finished their drinks and Tony tinkled the bell again and the waiter came again, this time more quickly. While they waited for his return, Tony walked to the restaurant door and the maître d'. Yes, they could have a table for two. The one there, at the end of the bar, would be all right? The table at the end of the bar is a choice one at the Algonquin. Sitting at it, one—or more likely two—can see whoever comes in. And, of course, be as easily seen, which to many has its points. In about ten minutes? Certainly, sir.

Tony went back to Rachel and they finished their drinks, not hurrying. Rachel put her glass down. She said, "One thing Janice told me I almost forgot. But probably it doesn't matter, hasn't got anything to do with anything. There's a woman named Barnes in this play Mr. Branson was starring in—*Summer* something, isn't it?—Helen Barnes, and a very good actress, Janice said. Character parts the last few years. Mother roles. That's what she is in the Branson play. Somebody's mother. Isn't that right?"

"The young wife's mother," Tony said. "What did Miss Towne tell you about her?"

"Well, she used to be married to Branson. Years ago, apparently. Only it didn't take, Janice doesn't know why. And I'm beginning to get hungry, I think."

At the table the captain was alert. Yes, they did care to order now. Certainly, Mr. Cook's roast beef would be rare. And a chef's salad for madame? But of course. And a martini for you, sir? Extra dry? And a twist, no olive. Yes, certainly.

"I thought you were hungry." Tony said. "A salad?"

"The way they make it here," Rachel said. "And are you sure you really need another drink?"

Tony was sure enough, although "need" was not precisely the word he would—

He stopped and looked at the youngish, slim man who had just come in from the lounge. The man hesitated just inside the dining room, only feet from their table. The maître d' greeted him. The maître d' said, "Good evening, Mr. Askew. Just one, sir?" to the author of *Summer Solstice*.

Askew merely nodded and was led down the long room. The maître d' pulled a single table away from the wall, and Askew sat on the banquette. A waiter was there at once.

"Bret Askew," Tony told Rachel. "He wrote the play Branson was in."

"Also," Rachel said, "he looked like being a little under the alfluence of incohol."

"Tee many martoonis," Tony said, completing the elderly gag.

The captain turned from the bar and put Tony's martini in front of him. Slivers of lemon peel came with it, in a small separate dish. The captain, Tony thought, had an excellent memory, or remarkable intuition. Tony twisted a lemon strip over his drink and rubbed it around the edge of the glass. But he did this automatically. He continued to look down the restaurant at Bret Askew, who was sitting very erectly on the banquette and who had both hands on the table.

"You could be right," Tony told Rachel.

He watched as Askew's waiter put a jigger containing bourbon, to judge from the color, on Askew's table, a glass with ice cubes in it, and a small pitcher of water.

Askew poured bourbon on the ice cubes. He ignored the water. If Askew was feeling no pain, he was, even more clearly, feeling no need for caution.

Tony looked thoughtfully at his own drink. It was just possible Rachel had a—his mind did not finish the sentence with its inevitable word. Movement by Askew interrupted it. The movement was the abrupt raising of the bourbon on rocks, the draining of it, the putting it down again on the table. Askew put his empty glass down hard, almost with violence. Then he pushed

76

the table away from him, that movement, too, abrupt; the table teetered a little. The waiter steadied it, perhaps just in time, and pulled it out, freeing Askew. The waiter said something, but Tony could only guess what. He could see Bret Askew shake his head. He also accepted the waiter's offered hand as he stood. Then he walked toward the front of the long room.

It could not be said that Askew staggered. But his gait was uncertain. Once, passing one of the central tables, he put a hand, obviously a steadying hand, on the back of one of its chairs. He came on toward the bar. When he reached it, he put his left hand on it and turned to face Rachel and Tony at their table. He leaned a little toward them, still clutching the bar.

"You're the police, aren't you?" Askew said. At least it sounded like that to Tony. Askew's voice, which had been sharply crisp and precise earlier in the day, was muffled now, just intelligible.

Tony said, "Yes, Mr. Askew."

"Something in my drink," Askew said. "Feel terri—n, He gave up on the word. He turned away and moved, still uncertainly, toward the entrance to the lobby.

There had been something in his drink—drinks—Tony thought. The something had been alcohol. Probably on an empty stomach. Probably drunk too fast, as he had gulped the one at the table. Tony watched the slim man walk toward the elevators, walking very carefully among the lounge tables, now all occupied. Of course, Askew had been under a strain. Everybody connected with *Summer Solstice* had had a day of strain. Askew, probably, had sought relaxation too ardently. Still—

His pupils had been dilated—very dilated. He had not only looked down at Tony, he had peered down, as if he were peering through a fog. Of course, excessive alcohol has effects which vary with individuals. With some it leads to clouding of the mind;

some it elates and some are depressed. And with some, motor impulses are interfered with, and they stagger. But dilation of the pupils? Tony did not know. He watched Askew go not too steadily into an elevator car.

"Well," Rachel said, "the poor guy." She made rather a point of looking fixedly at Tony's still barely touched martini.

Challenged, Tony sipped from it. But he only sipped. He put the glass down the width of the table away. Still, of course, within reach.

"Sorry," Rachel said. "Didn't mean to be wifely." She reached over and touched his hand. Tony closed his fingers around hers. The waiter brought their food then, and the captain served it. He mixed Rachel's salad in a wooden bowl and put only a part of it on her plate. He moved the salad bowl out of the way. It had been a good deal of salad. It contained strips of chicken and what Tony took to be ham. Chef's salads vary, presumably with chefs. Tony released Rachel's hand, freeing it for a fork.

Tony's roast beef was properly rare. The slice included the rib.

Tony took another sip of his martini, to prove nothing in particular—except that the drink was no longer very cold—and ate roast beef. But he thought of dilated pupils. Unsteady gait, mumbled speech, yes, of course. To be expected from a too hurried search for relaxation of nerves by the alcoholic route. A glassiness of eyes? Sometimes. But pupils so obviously dilated?

"You're letting your food get cold," Rachel told him. "Are you all right, Tony? Or have you gone back to working on this case of yours? Yours and Lieutenant Shapiro's?"

"Sorry," Tony said. "Salad all right?"

The salad was all right. It was fine. So, returned to, was the

78

rare roast beef. As they ate, they talked little. Over coffee, they talked, but not of murder. After Tony had signed the check he suggested brandy in the lounge. Rachel said, "Well—" doubt in her voice.

"After all," Tony said, "I never finished my cocktail."

"I'm sorry I sounded wifely," Rachel said again. "Cognac would be fine. You may have to carry me to the cab, of course."

There was a sofa free in the lounge. It faced the hotel desk, and the clerk behind it was a man Tony knew. Campbell. That was his name. Tony tinkled the bell and a waiter came.

"Two Martells," Tony said. "Not in snifters. And two small coffees."

The waiter said, "Sir," and went away.

"Would you like to be?" Tony said.

"What? Like to be what, dear?"

"Wifely," Tony said.

She looked at him for a moment, thoughtfully. "Not especial-ly," she said, after the pause. "We're all right the way we are. Aren't we?"

"We're fine the way we are," Tony said. "I just wondered."

"We're fine," Rachel said. "I like things the way they are. If I—well, if I change my mind I'll mention it. Probably."

Their drinks and coffee came. Tony signed for them and they sipped, sitting close together on the sofa, watching other people in the relaxing room. There was a couple in long dress and black tie, and the man looked, several times, at the watch on his wrist.

"Early for a party somewhere," Rachel said. "Killing time."

"Or heading for a first night," Tony said.

"I don't think there is any tonight," Rachel told him. "Any-way, people don't dress for them much anymore. And also, they'd be late."

It was true that New Yorkers no longer often dress for opening nights, and that early curtains prevail. And the big lounge clock showed eight forty.

They finished coffee and cognac, and Rachel raised inquiring eyebrows.

"I guess so," Tony said. "I would like to stop by the desk for a minute."

Rachel did not ask why. She merely nodded.

"Only a moment," Tony said, and got up and went to the desk and Mr. Campbell.

Campbell recognized him, but without any special enthusiasm. Cases have taken Tony to the Algonquin before. Police inquiries may be disturbing to hotels and possibly to hotel guests. Campbell said, "Good evening, Mr. Cook," his tone noticeably detached.

Tony said, "Evening," and, to put things on a more comfortable basis, "Nothing official, Mr. Campbell. Purely personal. Checking up on myself, you might put it. In my trade, you need to remember faces. Yours too, I'd think."

Melvin Campbell nodded. He said, "It helps. People like to be recognized."

"Sure," Tony said. "Thing is, Mr. Askew lives here, doesn't he? Bret Askew, the playwright?"

"Yes. Has a suite on the sixth floor. Why?"

"Happen to notice whether he was in the lounge this evening? Thing is, we've met several times, and I was pretty sure it was Askew came into the restaurant an hour or so ago. We, Miss Farmer and I, were sitting at the table by the bar, and he couldn't help seeing us. Looked right at us, matter of fact. And obviously didn't recognize me. No reason he should, of course; we're not palsy, anything like that. Still—well, I wondered whether my memory was going bad. Memory for faces, I mean.

80

I thought, maybe it wasn't Askew at all. See what I mean? Worrisome, sort of."

"Probably no reason to worry," Campbell said. "Probably was Mr. Askew. Anyway, he was in the lounge for a drink. I said good evening to him. Usually comes down around six thirty or so, has a quick one in the lounge, then goes into the restaurant. Not every night, of course. But pretty often. Did tonight, anyway. Could be he—well, had something on his mind. Thinking about something else and—well, didn't really see you, Mr. Cook. Friendly sort of guy, usually. Wait a minute. Didn't the star of this play of his die suddenly last night? Clive Branson. That was it, wasn't it? Branson, the movie actor?"

"I believe that's right," Tony said. "Probably upset Bret. Explain why he wasn't noticing much, wouldn't it? His first play on Broadway, he told me once. Counting on a big hit, probably. Well, relief to find out I'm not losing my memory for faces. Thanks for setting me straight, Mr. Campbell. In the lounge about seven, at a guess? Had a quick one and went in to eat."

"That's right. Only it wasn't such a quick one tonight. He had a friend with him. Man who lives here too. Called him up on the house phone, Mary says. The girl at the switchboard. Arranged for Mr. Price to have a drink with him. I was checking some people in about then. When I'd got them settled, I noticed Mr. Askew and Mr. Price were sitting over there. Where you and the lady have been sitting."

Tony turned and looked at the sofa. Rachel should have been on it. Rachel wasn't. For an instant, Tony was disturbed. Then she came out of the corridor which leads to, among other places, including the small barroom, the women's room. She started back toward the still-unoccupied sofa, but Tony said, "Rachel," and she joined him in front of the desk.

He said, "Apparently it was Bret Askew after all," which, understandably, meant nothing whatever to Rachel. She did not show that it meant nothing. "Had a drink with Price," Tony told her. He turned again to Campbell. "That was Ken Price, wasn't it?" he said. "The actor?"

"Yes," Campbell said, "Mr. Kenneth Price."

The telephone on his desk rang. He spoke into it. "Of course, Mary," he said. "Put Mr. Askew on."

9

Tony is a tall, lean man, not built for inconspicuous loitering in front of a hotel desk. But loitering, within earshot, seemed to be indicated. He whispered to Rachel, so softly that for a moment she looked as if she were about to say, "Huh?" She didn't. Obedient to what she had half heard, she went back to their table and tinkled its little bell. Not, she thought, that we really need another round.

Tony was not looking at her. He was looking at the opening of the corridor out of which she had just come, as if he were still waiting for a date to reappear.

"Can I help you, Mr. Askew?" Campbell said. "This is the front desk. Campbell, sir."

Then he listened. Tony could hear the rustle of a voice, but not the words in it.

"I'm very sorry, Mr. Askew," the desk clerk said. "On vacation, you say? Never around when we need them, are they?" As if, Tony thought, Askew were asking for a policeman.

"No, Mr. Askew, we don't have a house physician. Not what you'd call that. But there is a doctor we can call on sometimes when guests need one. A Dr. Knight. Has offices across the street. I can—" He stopped abruptly. "The doctor is just coming through the lobby," he told the telephone. "I'll ask him." He raised his voice a little. He said, "Oh, Doctor Knight."

83

The man he summoned was not knightly in appearance. He was rather short and somewhat pudgy. He was not carrying a doctor's black bag. But he said, "Yes?"

"One of our guests isn't feeling well," Campbell said. "Would like you to have a look at him. A regular guest, Doctor. Suite Six-oh-one, Mr. Askew."

"After office hours," Knight said. "A hell of a lot. What does he think's the matter with him? Stomachache?"

"He just says he feels queer," Campbell said. "But if you wouldn't mind, Doctor. He's a playwright. Lived here for several months."

Dr. Knight said, "Hmm," as if he didn't think much of playwrights. But he went to the elevators.

Tony heard Campbell tell the telephone, "The doctor is on his way up." He went back to their table and sat again beside Rachel. After a few minutes a waiter brought their cognacs. They sipped and waited, waited for about half an hour, Tony with his eyes on the elevators. Finally, Dr. Knight came out of one of them. He went to the desk and, rather briefly, talked to Campbell. Then he went out of the hotel. Campbell tapped the desk bell, and a bellman responded. The bellman got instructions. They led him across the lobby, among the tables already beginning to fill for the after-theater buffet. He stopped in front of Tony and Rachel. He said, "Mr. Cook, sir?" Tony admitted it. Would he come to the desk for a moment, sir?

Tony finished his cognac and went to the desk.

"It's Mr. Askew, Mr. Cook," Campbell said. "He asked whether you were still in the hotel, and if you were, would you come up and see him. What he said was, 'I want to report something.' I'm not sure what he meant."

Tony wasn't either. He said, "I take it he's feeling better?"

84

Bret Askew hadn't mentioned how he was feeling. He was in Suite 601. You went left down the corridor from the elevator. Tony went back to the table and explained to Rachel, who said "Damn!" She finished her drink. She said, "You can put me in a cab, mister." She almost never called him "mister" anymore. He was sorry about it. He would be along as soon as he could.

"All right," Rachel said. "It's what I get for going around with a policeman. Stood up. I ought to be getting used to it." Then she smiled at him. "I don't deny there are compensations, Tony," she said.

He put her in a cab, which was readily available. Cabs were dropping supper people at the Algonquin.

Tony Cook went up to the sixth floor and, to the left, along the corridor. It ended in a closed door with "601" on it. Tony knocked on the door and heard "Come in," in a rather hoarse voice.

Bret Askew was in shirt sleeves, his shirt open at the neck. He was sitting in a chair, with a coffee cup on a table beside him. There was also a coffeepot on the table, and Askew refilled his cup. There was only one cup, but plenty of coffee. If Detective Cook wanted to join him, he could get a glass from the bathroom. Tony didn't.

"Supposed to keep pouring it down," Askew said, "What this doctor told me to do. Said I ought to go to the hospital and have stomach lavage, but I'd come along all right with caffeine. At least, he was pretty sure I would."

He drank from his refilled cup. "They do send you up good coffee," he said. He still sounded hoarse, as if his throat were dry. His pupils were still dilated.

"Thing is," Askew said, "apparently somebody tried to kill me. Didn't use enough of the stuff, luckily for me . . . just the four tenths of a milligram or so you'd get in a prescription. Maybe a little more. Takes a good many times that if you want to be sure, you know."

"The stuff?" Tony said. "You know what this stuff was? The doctor told you?"

"More like I told him," Askew said. "He agreed I probably was right. Said the symptoms fitted and that the only way to be sure was to have my stomach pumped out. But that he was pretty sure I'd be all right—the symptoms weren't all that extreme. Blurred vision, dryness of the throat, some burning sensation, but nothing too bad. And that a lot of coffee ought to help. Whoever put it in my drink hadn't done his research, is what it comes to."

"Look, Mr. Askew," Tony said, "so far it hasn't come to anything. Not to me, anyway. What do you think was put into your drink?"

"One of the alkaloids. Belladonna group, probably atropine sulfate. Doctors do prescribe it. Sometimes, anyway. Not as often as they used to, this doctor says, but sometimes, to check excess secretions. For ulcers of the stomach, mostly. And for irritable colon, Dr. Knight says. You ever been to an eye doctor, Cook? They put stuff in your eyes to dilate the pupils. So they can look in."

Tony had been to an ophthalmologist. He hadn't needed glasses. "This atropine?" he said.

"One of the related alkaloids. They come from plants, you know. Atropine from deadly nightshade. Kids eat berries from it. Enough berries and *poof*—no more kid."

"You seem to know a good deal about this poison," Tony said. "But the point is, how it got into your glass. That's why you wanted to see me, I take it."

"Couple–three years ago I was working on a play. Mystery—mystery comedy, you'd have to call it. I looked up some poisons for it. Only the damn thing never would jell. Sometimes they do, somethimes they don't. Happens in your line of work too, I shouldn't wonder. I don't know how it got into my glass, Cook. Job for the police, I'd figure."

To whom, Bret Askew was not, at the moment, being of any great help. He was hard to pin down.

"What drink?" Tony asked. "And where, do you think?"

"Double martini. In the lounge, I suppose, where I was having a before-dinner drink."

"With Kenneth Price, I understand."

"Yes. How'd you know?"

"Desk clerk told me; said you called Price up. Asked him to join you in the lounge. It was your idea, apparently."

"Yes. About the reading of a line in the second act. He's taking over for poor old Branson, you know."

"Yes, I know he's taking the role Clive Branson had."

"Damn bad thing about Branson. Rumor around he took an overdose. Bad thing all around. Bad for the play, bad for Rolf Simon, and probably bad for me. Looked like it was rolling. Now, who knows?"

"To get back to what we were talking about, Mr. Askew. This alkaloid in your drink; how it got there. What is it? A liquid?"

"Granular powder, the book says. Probably dispensed in capsules. Never been given it myself. Haven't got an ulcer, apparently. God knows why, the trade I'm in. You could call ulcers an occupational hazard, I guess. For all writers, but playwrights most of all. Will it get produced? Will the actors get the faintest idea what you were shooting at? Will the critics? Crickets, Edwin Booth used to call them. In spite of the fact that they gave him raves. Not a bad line for an actor. Will it run. Sure we get ulcers."

"But you haven't. And so never had this drug—atropine sulfate, you think—prescribed by your doctor. Who isn't Dr. Knight, I take it."

"Hell, no. Never saw him before. Dr. Benjamin's my man. Dr. Cyrus Benjamin. Funny combination of names, wouldn't you say? Sure you don't want some coffee while it's still warm?" He poured coffee into his cup and drank a little of it. "Well," he said, "warmish, anyway."

Tony Cook was sure he didn't want coffee. He wanted Bret Askew to stick to one subject, if only for a moment. He was beginning to give up hope he'd ever get what he wanted. "You asked Mr. Price to come down to the lobby and have a drink with you. And to talk about his reading of a line."

"Several lines, actually. In the first act, and the second and third, come to that."

"You aren't satisfied with the way he's playing the part?"

"I wouldn't go that far. Another Clive Branson he isn't. But who is? The run-through this afternoon was O.K. Seemed so to me, anyway. Oh, Kirby was sort of fussy, but I thought it went all right. Ken went up a couple of times, but nothing to worry about."

"You and Mr. Price sat at one of the tables in the lounge and had your drinks. And talked about the way he was reading lines. And you think it was while you two were having your drinks that somebody put this alkaloid in your glass. Broke open a capsule, probably, and sifted this powder into your martini. And— Mr. Price was closest, wasn't he? At the same table."

"At the same table. But it wasn't Ken. I'd have seen him. Anyway, why would he?"

88

"Why would anyone, Mr. Askew? You any idea about that?"

"No. Hell, no. Nobody's got it in for me. Why would anybody have? What I do is sit in a room with a typewriter and write plays. No harm to anybody. Maybe no good to anybody, either. What I'm getting at—I don't get around much, and if you don't get around you don't bump into people, do you?"

"This evening, while you and Mr. Price were having drinks, did you see anybody you knew in the lounge?"

"Knew by sight. I have dinner here rather often, and a drink in the lounge first. So do a good many people. Theater people, writers, that sort. You get to know faces. Even get to nodding at people you don't really know. If you mean, people I do really know, no, I don't remember any this evening. Friends *or* enemies. Not, as I just said, that I have any enemies I know of. Oh, Martha came in. Martha Abel, the agent. Ken was expecting her, he'd told me when I suggested our getting together for a drink. We were sitting where we could see when she came in. On a sofa across the lounge from the desk."

"The one near the dining-room entrance, Mr. Askew?"

"Yes. One of the ones, anyway."

"So people going in to dinner would walk close to it?"

"I suppose so. But, no, Cook. I didn't see anybody I really know. Friend or foe."

"You and Mr. Price had drinks. What did you have, by the way?"

"Martini. Up. Ken had bourbon on the rocks, way I remember it. I was just starting on my second when Martha showed up. We both saw her, and both stood up. Ken sort of waved and she came over. I said wouldn't she join us, but she said she and Ken had to be getting along."

"Your drinks were on the table while you were talking to Mrs. Abel?"

"Sure, I guess so. Hell, man. Who remembers every move? Every detail?"

"Nobody, I suppose. Did you have your back to the table while you were talking to Mrs. Abel.? Asking her to join you?"

"Could be. You mean, could she have put the stuff in my drink without my seeing her? I suppose she could have. But—having a capsule of atropine handy? Just on the chance she might want to poison somebody? Come off it, Cook. She didn't even know I'd be with Ken. How could she have?"

Ken Price could have told her, after he had agreed to meet Askew in the lounge for a drink and a few words about the reading of lines, Tony thought. But didn't say.

Was there anything else about his session with Price that Askew could remember? Anything that, looked back on, stood out, seemed a little odd? Askew shook his head. His movements, now, seemed more certain, his voice less strained.

Askew poured from the coffeepot again. Half a cup emptied the pot. He got up from the chair, having no apparent difficulty, and went across the room to the telephone on the bedside table. The bed was a couch. Instead of returning to his chair, Askew sat on the couch. He leaned back on cushions propped against the wall and used the telephone to order a pot of coffee from room service.

Then he said, "I don't remember anything, Cook. We talked. I read a couple of lines to show him what I meant, what I'd meant when I wrote them. One requires a little action, and I stood up and walked a couple of steps while I read it."

"Back to the table? And Mr. Price?"

"Maybe—I was thinking about the line. How I'd meant it to be said. Anyway, it was only a couple of steps, to show the business I wanted. A couple of seconds, at the outside. Then—wait a minute—Ken got up and read it my way, with the business I'd

90

asked for. And said, yes, he saw what I was driving at. And he'd remember at the next run-through, which will be tomorrow morning. I'll be sitting in, if I'm up to it. Smooth out rough spots in the script, if any show up. What I've been doing all along. Tomorrow afternoon, too probably. Simon wants to open again tomorrow night, you know; wants to get McClay to cover it—to cover Price in it, actually. And wants the Drummond dame too, of course. Though the *Chronicle* is the one that counts. It's McClay carries the weight, you know. The *Sentinel*—well." He shrugged.

Tony didn't, precisely. He nodded his head to show he did.

"Mrs. Abel showed up, but wouldn't join the two of you for a drink. Then?"

Price had taken the final sip of his bourbon on the rocks, and he and Martha Abel had left the hotel. Askew had half a martini left and had finished it and had begun to feel "a little funny." He had gone into the dining room and been taken to a table. No, he hadn't noticed Tony Cook and Rachel at the table at the end of the bar. Not then. He had started to order and found there was something the matter with his throat. "Seemed to have dried up, you know." He had decided to go up to his room and lie down for a bit instead of having dinner.

"You remember seeing Miss Farmer and me on your way out?"

"Not all that clearly. Remembered, pretty vaguely, when I was up here. And began to get a hunch about what was the matter with me. And tried to get my regular doctor, and discovered he was on vacation. He'd arranged for a stand-in, but I couldn't get hold of him, either, so I asked the desk to send somebody. They sent Dr. Knight. After he more or less confirmed what I'd guessed, I remembered, half remembered, seeing you. Sort of in a blur. And I—well, I thought maybe I'd better report what had

91

happened. Not that it had anything to do with what happened to poor Clive Branson."

The coffee came. A pot of it, and a fresh cup. And cream and sugar. Askew thanked and tipped the waiter, who said, "Thank *you*, sir," and took the used cup and empty pot away. Askew served himself coffee and said, "Sure you won't join me?"

Tony remained sure he wouldn't have coffee. He said, "Speaking of Branson, you were at this surprise birthday party Mr. Simon gave for him, I understand?"

"Sure. Everybody connected with the play. Except the stage hands, anyway. Doesn't come under their contract. Damn near everything else does, you know. Have to get a special ruling if we want an actor to—hell, move a chair on the set. But they don't have to be invited to staff parties." He drank from his cup. It was a little as if he were biting the cup. He said, "It was a nice, easygoing party. Until old Clive started emptying ashtrays, anyway. Half asleep on his feet, the old boy seemed to be."

"Before that, Mr. Askew. Anything out of the way? Anything you noticed?"

"I don't know what you're after, I'm afraid. Oh! Did I see somebody put poison in Branson's glass? So somebody kill the old boy?"

"We don't know yet. It's possible. Somebody who knew Branson was more than normally susceptible to sleeping medicine. To all the barbiturates. Did you happen to know that, Mr. Askew?"

"No, I didn't happen to know that, Mr. Cook. Or anything else about Branson, except that he was supposed to be one hell of an actor, and that Simon wanted him for *Summer Solstice*. If he could get him. Which, I gather, was chancy up to the last go-round. With him and Abel. He came high, I gather."

"Any idea how high, Mr. Askew?"

"Not my department, Cook. My royalty is on the gross. At a

guess, could have been several thousand a week. Maybe ten, for all I know. So, stick the customers. Which is O.K. with me, naturally. Long as they come, that is. Twenty a throw for the orchestra seats. Man! Does that shove up the gross! Which is where I come in. Did come in, anyway. With Branson out of the cast, God knows."

He brooded for some seconds over his coffee.

"If you're thinking somebody's been trying to shut me up, Cook, shut me up with atropine, it's out. Nothing to be shut up about. Because I didn't see anybody put sleeping medicine in Branson's drink. Or anything else out of the way. At this damn party or any other time."

Tony said, "All right, Mr. Askew. I'll turn in a report." He left the playwright's sixth-floor, two-room suite and went down to the lobby and to a telephone booth.

10

He dialed the number of the Hotel Algonquin. When he was answered, from a few feet away, he said, "Mr. Price, please. Mr. Kenneth Price." He heard the repeated buzz which indicated a telephone bell was ringing in Price's rooms. Ringing and not being answered. Then he was told that Mr. Price did not seem to be in his suite.

He dialed Homicide South and reported an apparent effort to poison Bret Askew, playwright. And reported that Askew seemed little the worse for the attempt, which might, he thought, be in some manner related to the more successful effort to do away with Clive Branson, actor. He was told that Lieutenant Shapiro had signed out and had also signed Cook out. He was asked if he needed somebody to lend a hand. Tony didn't. He would try to get in touch with Shapiro and fill him in. He dialed a familiar Brooklyn number, and the telephone rang in the apartment of Rose and Nathan Shapiro, and rang unanswered. It was a night of elusive people. He looked up Abel, Martha, in the directory. Two listings—"Abel Martha Associates. Abel Martha res." He tried the latter. After four rings, it was answered—"Mrs. Abel's apartment"—via, clearly, an answering service. No, Tony did not wish to leave a number.

He looked up another number and dialed again. John Knight, M.D., would almost certainly not be in his office, which apparently was more or less across Forty-fourth Street from the Hotel Algonquin.

But he was. The answer was abrupt, in a low, somewhat grating voice, the voice of a man who did not much want to be disturbed. "Knight speaking."

"Dr. Knight?"

"John Knight, M.D."

"This is the police, Doctor. Detective Cook."

"All right. And so what?"

"You treated a man this evening in the Algonquin. A Mr. Askew. Mr. Bret Askew. Right?"

"I wouldn't say treated. Looked in on. Pretty much confirmed his own diagnosis. Seemed to know a good deal about it. Said he had researched for a play awhile back. Had all the symptoms down pat, anyway."

"Symptoms of, Doctor?"

"Poisoning by one of the alkaloids, belladonna group. Probably atropine sulfate, he thought."

"And he was right?"

"The symptoms were right. Blurred vision, dilation of the pupils, dry throat and some fuddled speech. Conformed to poisoning by atropine. All I had to go on. I'd have to take him to a hospital for tests to be sure. He wouldn't go. Didn't want his stomach pumped out, I suppose. Can't blame him, can you? Anyway, he was coming out of it. I told him to drink a lot of coffee, figured he'd be all right in a few hours. Wait a minute! You mean he isn't? That he's—well, died of it?"

"No, Doctor. Nothing like that. Seemed to be coming along all right. Only he's filed a report. Thinks somebody tried to poison him. Dropped this alkaloid in his drink. In the Algonquin lounge."

"What he told me, too."

95

"And, Doctor, something you're required to report. Have you?"

"Not yet. Planned to in the morning. O.K.? Or—You say you're a detective. So, it's already been reported, huh? By this man Askew himself, you say. So?"

"You'd better report it anyway, Doctor. As, perhaps, attempted murder."

"All right. In the morning. But a pretty feeble attempt, Cook. You did say your name is Cook? A mild overdose of a drug used to curb excessive secretions. For peptic ulcer, sometimes. Or an irritated colon. Had to look the stuff up myself when I got back here. Never prescribed it myself, that I remember."

"But it is prescribed?"

"Yes. Some internists use it. It will also dry up a runny cold. Pretty drastic treatment for that, though."

"Since you've just looked it up, Doctor—on the assumption that it was atropine sulfate—what would be the usual dosage?"

"Four tenths of a milligram. Repeated after four hours. A fraction, small fraction, of the presumed fatal dose."

"Any idea how much Askew was given? Or, of course, took?"

"Not more than twice the therapeutic dose. At a guess. I told you he wouldn't go for a thorough test. And I couldn't drag him, could I? And I was pretty sure he wasn't going to die of it."

"Could be his doctor prescribed it for him and he just took too much?"

"Could be, I suppose. But he denied ever having a prescription for it. Yes, I thought of the possibility, and asked him."

"Yes, Doctor. Any chance he could—well, have faked the symptoms?"

"Try dilating your own pupils sometime, Cook. No, he'd had the stuff, all right. Perhaps not atropine. Could be one of the

96

others in the belladonna group. Never know, will we? And, all right, I'll file a report in the morning. Pretty sketchy report it will be, though."

Tony said it would be a good idea to file a report, if just to keep the record straight. "Thank you, Doctor." He hung up. He tried once more to get Lieutenant Shapiro in Brooklyn and again had no success.

Poison in the drinks of two men. Overdoses, actually, of reasonably standard medications. One fatal because of the special susceptibility of the victim; the other merely an annoyance. A play, and a light comedy at that, the link between the two men. And the lieutenant away somewhere. At a movie? Damn! Perhaps Kenneth Price had returned, would be available to tell of his brief drinking session with Askew and, of course, to deny he had sprinkled atropine sulfate into Askew's glass. Probably to deny he had ever heard of atropine sulfate.

Tony had run out of dimes and used one of the house telephones. If Price was in his suite, he was not answering his telephone.

Outside the hotel, Tony succumbed to the temptation of a just-vacated taxi. It would have been more sensible to go downtown by subway. Tony was not feeling very sensible.

The taxi driver had never heard of Gay Street. He seemed barely to have heard of Greenwich Village. He said, "Oh, *Green*wich." Tony paid him off at Sixth Avenue and Ninth Street and walked the rest of the way, to save time.

There was a streak of light under the door of Rachel's second-floor apartment, as Tony had hoped there would be. She answered quickly to his ring. She even had clothes on.

"There's nothing like having a dinner date with a policeman," she said. "Is that man who stared at us dead?"

97

"No. Very alive and kicking. Name of Askew. Man who wrote *Summer Solstice*." He let go of her and told her, briefly, about Askew's uncomfortable experience.

"First the actor, then the playwright," Rachel said. "Somebody's certainly got it in for that play. All right, Tony love, I'll take it off. All right, you can help if you want to."

* * * * *

It was some time later, and in the bed of his own apartment, that Tony Cook wakened. Momentarily, he was surprised to be in his own bed, alone. Then he remembered. Rachel and Tony are rather often in bed together, but seldom for sleeping. They quickly become too conscious of each other for sleep. So, what had wakened him at—he looked—four thirty in the morning? Something that kept tumbling around in his mind. After a few seconds it came to him. Something Rachel had said just before he helped her off with the dress.

"Somebody's got it in for the play." Which was certainly nothing to wake up about. A slight but witty comedy, it was said to be. A little reminiscent of Noel Coward. Nothing anybody would have it in for. Unless—

Tony's father had been an ardent playgoer, although usually in the balcony. And once, Tony had heard him say that somebody "could sue the ass off her, only the somebody's dead." Tony had known his father was talking about a play and had asked for more.

He had got it. It was a play written by a woman and very obviously about her late husband, whose name she still bore. It had been, by general agreement, a very witty play and an entirely merciless one. The husband, who had been well known—chiefly for the amount of money he owned—had been ridiculed as a man of barely credible stupidity, a sluggish bore, inept in all things, including lovemaking. "She really took the skin off him.

98

He would have rolled over in his grave, except he'd been cremated."

Partly the wit, and to a degree the malice, had made the play a success. One of the reviewers had written that he loathed it and that it probably would run forever. It hadn't, but it had run well and been, briefly, mentioned in connection with the Pulitzer Prize, which it had not received.

Tony could not remember the title of the play or the name of its author. But a good many people, including relatives of the obvious prototype, might well have had a grudge against it. And tried to do it in?

Unlikely, of course. Unlikely as hell. Still, it went to show you could certainly have a grudge against a play—and against its author. Try to stop it by temporarily incapacitating its leading actor? Not, probably, intending the incapacity to be permanent? And then to punish the author, not intending to kill him?

It hardly held water. It did not justify being waked up at four thirty in the morning. Still—had there been a prototype for a character in Askew's play? Some actual person who felt that the play "really took the skin off him"? Farfetched, of course. But possible? Worth looking into? Something to query Askew about, conceivably.

Clearly not at four thirty in the morning, but it took Tony Cook fifteen minutes to get back to sleep.

11

Cleo is usually happy about mornings and greets them with pleased noises. This happens at seven o'clock, give or take a few minutes, and the time of advent does not vary with the time of year or the intensity of the light. For Cleo, morning is seven o'clock.

After her preliminary greetings, probably intended to reassure morning it is welcome, Cleo hurries to a chair by the apartment's east living-room window. On it, she repeats her greeting, more emphatically than before. Then it is time to let out her charges, who have been shut up for the night. Letting them out is the first order of morning business. Then she will take the longer of her charges for his morning walk. That can be protracted as befits the weather. Breakfast will surely follow. Indeed, it never fails.

This morning started out like any other, with sounds of welcome, with the dash to the window chair. But instead of gleeful yelps, Cleo made a sound which was almost a whimper. She repeated this several times before she went to the door they were shut behind to let them out, to let them share her disappointment and chagrin, for which they are, after all, responsible. She lets them out by scratching at their door and barking at it. Only this time it was more whimper than bark. Cleo does not like to walk in the rain.

Nathan Shapiro doesn't either, but there is no alternative. Dogs have to be walked.

Cats are another and simpler matter. Early in their married life, they had learned that the chance of their having children was one in—"well, about one in five thousand," Dr. Horowitz had told Nathan "Probably the mumps you had when you were twenty. Too bad—but just be thankful that mumps in men doesn't affect potency." Being duly thankful, they had tried a cat, a sleek and friendly Siamese, and Rose had turned out to be, rather violently, allergic to cats. So they had had to find a new home for Chin, with a family who didn't sneeze and wheeze because of her presence. Dogs were chancy, too, people who are sensitive to cat dander often react adversely to dogs also—even to ponies, for that matter—but Rose got along all right with dogs, and Cleo was their third scottie. Their first dog had been a dachshund, who had been most amiable despite his Germanic association. But the Shapiros, while by no means orthodox, had felt that a Germanic dog was inappropriate in the Hitler era, and had switched to Scotch terriers. Cleo is the third of that breed to live with, and be taken for walks by, Rose and Nathan Shapiro.

From Cleo's mournful response this morning, Nathan had inferred an adverse change in the weather even before he looked toward the window and got up rather hurriedly to close it. The almost-summer weather had indeed broken. It needn't have been quite so emphatic about it, Nathan thought. The rain was slashing down in sheets. It was by no means a warm rain. Nathan Shapiro, who shares Cleo's distaste for walking in the rain, sighed as he went into the bathroom. The window was open there, too. The rain was pouring in.

Rose said from her bed, "Raining, isn't it?"

Nathan said it was raining. Hard.

Rose said, "Damn." Then she said, "Anyway, I'm glad it's morning." Nathan walks Cleo in the mornings. Rose has the afternoon shift.

Cleo scratched at the bedroom door. She was not very vigorous at it. It was rather as if she hoped not to be heard.

Nathan opened the door. He said, "Good morning, Cleo." Cleo answered on a subdued note. She put paws up against a pajama leg and looked up, sorrowfully, at Nathan's face. "Yes," Nathan said, "I know it is. No doing of mine, dog."

Cleo whined a rejection of this obvious untruth.

"Go get it," Nathan told the little bitch.

Cleo never has to be told to get her lead and bring it to be snapped to her collar. Except on rainy mornings. She did go and get it. She dropped it at some distance from her long one, teaching him not to make it rain.

Shapiro went back to the bedroom and dressed. Rose went into the bathroom. She was out of it by the time her husband had finished with his necktie.

"Don't let her stall you, dear," Rose said. "And do take an umbrella." Cleo often protracts her morning walks.

"She won't today," Nathan said. "Not in this." He didn't say anything about taking an umbrella. He detests umbrellas. He finished dressing. He put on a raincoat and a hat, which is reserved for rainy days. He put folded sheets of yesterday's New York *Chronicle* in the pocket of the raincoat. A local law requires New York City dog owners to clean up after their pets. Police Lieutenant Shapiro is, of course, a lawman. On better days, Cleo pulls Nathan out the apartment door. Today, he had, gently, to pull her. She did not seriously resist. She was resigned, if not enthusiastic. At the rain-swept curb, she did not dilly-dally.

They were back in the apartment in ten minutes, and in eleven Nathan was drinking the coffee Rose had ready for him. She let him drink half the cup while she fed Cleo, whose spirits were improving. Then Rose came in carrying her own cup and sat beside him on the sofa facing the fireplace, for which they would soon have to buy wood. Rabbi Shapiro, Nathan's father, smiled down at them from the portrait above the mantel. He had been a smiling man as well as a learned one.

"Tony Cook called," Rose told her husband. "Would like you to call him back before you go in?"

Nathan finished his coffee and stood up.

"Not until you've had your egg," Rose told him. For Nathan Shapiro, breakfast is something one drinks from a coffee cup. He waited for his soft-boiled egg. He even ate it. Then he looked at his watch. Almost a quarter of eight. Cook would be in transit between Gay Street and the headquarters of Homic le, Manhattan South. Lieutenant Nathan Shapiro, short of a miracle, would not check in by eight o'clock. His tardiness would offend no one.

He accepted a refill of his coffee cup. He lighted a cigarette. And the telephone rang. Nathan went to answer it. Rose had already answered on the kitchen extension. She said, "Yes, Tony, he is", and Nathan cut in.

Tony said, "Morning, Nate," which meant he was not calling from the squad room. There it would have been "Good morning, Lieutenant." Or even "Sir." Tony was glad he had caught Shapiro before he left for the office. Because—

Shapiro listened to Tony's report on last night's episode of Bret Askew and the atropine. Yes, he'd heard of atropine. . . . Tony had failed to get hold of Ken Price; had got Martha Abel's answering service but no Martha Abel. But had talked with Dr. John Knight . . . and had tried Price again this morning, so far without success. Sure, they'd have to keep on trying.

103

"Thing is," Tony said, "they won't ring his room before ten. After they've sent his breakfast up. Strict orders from a valued guest. No exceptions. . . . Sure, I told them it was a police matter, Nate. . . . No, I didn't make it urgent—no use scaring him off, way I figured it. And after all, lots of people in that lobby at the time, and moving around a lot. Also, precinct's got a man standing by. Cleared that with the cap—I mean inspector. Just to be sure. So I thought we might—"

"Yes," Shapiro said. "I'll meet you there, Tony. In the lobby. . . . Oh, half an hour or so. Turn up anything else after we split, Tony? Miss Farmer help?"

He listened.

Jason Abel? Sure he'd heard of him; who hadn't? A million settlement, at a guess? Nice for Martha as a divorced wife. He agreed it would leave her free to pick and choose among clients, and also, of course, make the need of valuable clients less pressing. Sure, they'd bear it in mind.

"And speaking of ex-wives," Tony said, "there's one of Clive Branson's in the cast of *Summer Solstice*. Helen Barnes, her name is. Plays the mother. Seems like a hell of a note."

Shapiro agreed it was a hell of a note. Sure, domestic relationships, even past ones, did tend to louse things up. One more item to bear in mind . . . and yes, just now the rain was lousing things up. If Inspector Weigand approved, a squad car from precinct would be most welcome. Even if it wasn't all that urgent. O.K., he'd see Tony at the Algonquin in half an hour or so.

Dr. Rose Shapiro also had office hours to keep, at a high school in Greenwich Village. But Rose, who cannot be transported in a police car, has a tame taxi driver, tame even on rainy mornings, so both of them could get to work without getting too wet. Cleo watched them go. She was not happy about it. She never is. After they had left, she went to her favorite chair, which is forbidden her.

The Algonquin lobby is not active at eight thirty in the mornings. It is usually deserted. It was this morning when Shapiro went into it. A couple, probably Middle Westerners, were checking out. Bellmen hovered over their considerable collection of luggage. The restaurant was almost as empty as the lobby. Algonquin guests commonly breakfast in their rooms, and seldom as early as eight thirty. The morning desk clerk was not a man Tony Cook knew.

No, Mr. Price could not be rung in his suite at this hour. Never before ten. Mr. Price was most explicit about that. Certainly never before room service had supplied his breakfast. Yes, he understood that that was usually at a few minutes after ten. Whenever Mr. Price called down for it, of course. No, he could not see that an exception had to be made for police officers. Yes, he was reasonably certain Mr. Price had not left his suite. Or the hotel. He never did at this hour. Well, he supposed he could check with the housekeeper, although the maid was instructed not to disturb Mr. Price early. Certainly not at this—all right, if the lieutenant insisted. The desk clerk used the telephone. Mrs. Grady? Had there by any chance been a change in the morning routine as regarded Mr. Price? Yes, Suite Five-oh-one . . . Maria Perotti? Yes, he would like to see her, if she could be sent down. Sorry to be a nuisance.

"Seems Mr. Price did leave early this morning," the clerk told Shapiro and Cook. It was most unusual. He had been in the hall when the maid, a Maria Perotti, came out of a room across the corridor which she had just done up. He had asked her to do his rooms early.

Maria Perotti was young and reasonably pretty. She was

105

neatly uniformed. She said, "Sir?" to the desk clerk. Of course, sir, she would answer any questions the gentlemen wished to ask, if she could, about Mr. Price in Suite Five-oh-one—she called it "suit"—not that she knew anything about Mr. Price. This morning was the first time she had ever seen him. About half an hour ago. Well, he had come out of the suite.

"He said good morning, and was I the one who took care of his room? I said I was, and was everything all right? About the rooms, I meant. He said everything was fine and that he hoped the time he insisted on didn't break up my schedule."

"The time, Miss Perotti?"

"Never do the suit before eleven in the morning. And have it done by noon, if that was all right. I told him it worked out just fine. As it does, Lieutenant, sir. Five-thirteen usually goes downstairs for breakfast, you know, around half-past, so I can do that one and get to Five-ninety-one at a few minutes after eleven. Five-oh-one's always out by then. And there's never any trouble about his rooms, no mess or anything. Not like some, I can tell you. Just do up the beds and put out the towels and run the vac. Maybe fifteen minutes, all told. Very nice gentleman, Mr. Price is. And a dollar every other day, regular as clockwork. Ever since he moved in last summer, if you know what I mean."

"Yes, Miss Perotti. This morning was different, you say. Tell us about this morning."

"I had a couple of checkouts and I'd just finished with them. I was just about to knock at Five-oh-two—it's across the hall from Five-oh-one—and Mr. Price came out of Five-oh-one and said good morning and was I the one who did his rooms, and if I was I could do them anytime because he was going out early."

"He was dressed for going out?" Tony asked.

Price had been dressed for going out. In suit and necktie. "He had a raincoat over his arm."

106

"Carrying anything else?"

"Not that I noticed, sir. Only I thought—think now, anyway—he might have had something under the raincoat, something—oh, brown, sort of."

"Like a briefcase, Miss Perotti?"

"It could have been that, I guess. Something brown and—well, flat. Under the raincoat."

"Yes, Miss Perotti. And then?"

"Then?"

"What happened then?"

"Oh. He went down the corridor toward the elevators, and I went in and did the suit. If you can call it that. All it needed was fresh towels."

"And made up the bed, I suppose?"

"Not fresh—that is, it wasn't the day to change the sheets. Not in five-oh-one. We—"

"With resident guests we change the bed linen every other day, Lieutenant," the desk clerk said, "unless the guest requests otherwise."

Shapiro said he saw. So the maid had merely made up Mr. Price's bed without changing anything?

"Not even that sir—both beds were made already up. It was like he—like he hadn't slept in his room last night. Unless, of course, he made up the bed himself, but, why should he? He never did. And anyway, it looked just like it did when I finished with it yesterday."

So. A change in Price's routine. To avoid inquiries by the police? Rather obvious about it, in that case. As if he was calling attention to something. Have a look at Price's suite to see if their attention had been called to something? Probably not worth the trouble, or the time.

"While we're here, Tony," Shapiro said, "we might check on

107

Askew, find out how he's feeling. Unless it's against the rules to disturb him this early?"

The desk clerk answered that. Mr. Askew never stipulated a time before which he should not be called. In general, of course, they tried not to have guests awakened at inconvenient hours. And there were not many early risers among the Algonquin's clientele. Still—the house phones were at the end of the desk.

"I wonder," Tony Cook said, "whether we might have a look through Mr. Price's suite? Just—well, to see if he perhaps left a message. And—well, to make sure he didn't take his clothes with him this morning."

The clerk made sounds of indignation. Mr. Price was a long-time and highly respected guest. He also made noises about a search warrant.

"Oh," Tony said, "nothing formal like that. Just a quick look around, with Miss Perotti or someone along if you like."

The desk clerk was not pleased. Probably he ought to consult the manager. But at this hour? Well, he supposed there would be no real harm in it. Miss Perotti could let them in; go in with them, he supposed.

"Go along, Tony," Shapiro said. "I'll give Mr. Askew a buzz. See how he's feeling this morning."

Shapiro went to the house phones. The operator would ring Mr. Askew, sir. In Suite 601. One moment, please.

She rang three times without an answer. She was afraid—she rang a fourth time.

"I'm afraid Mr. Askew isn't in, sir." No, there hadn't been any calls for him that morning. Not since she came on. She came on at eight. From him? No. Oh, except to room service. At about a quarter after eight, she thought it was. Yes, Mr. Askew usually had breakfast sent up to his suite. Well, usually not quite this early. But before nine, almost every morning. "Thank *you*, sir."

108

Nathan went to one of the telephone booths and consulted the Manhattan directory. He found the two listings Tony had undoubtedly found last night and dialed the number for "Abel Martha res."

"Mrs. Abel's residence." Mrs. Abel was in the shower the voice said. Could she take a message? Lieutenant Shapiro? Of the police? Well . . .

"Good morning, Lieutenant. . . . Yes, it is—dripping wet at the moment. . . . Yes, of course he's a client and, yes, a friend. He lives at the Algonquin—oh, you're there and he isn't? . . . Well, anywhere, for all I know." Yes, he had stopped by her place last night—for a drink. Had left—oh, a little after midnight, at a guess. She hadn't the foggiest where he had gone then—back to the Algonquin, she supposed. "Yes, it is early for him to be up and about. After all, he's an actor, and they're not precisely—oh, wait a minute, Lieutenant. Wait a minute. What time is it?"

It was around nine thirty.

"Then he's at the theater, or on his way there. Early rehearsal, for the reopening tonight. They're trying to get the critics back, you know. Mr. Simon's idea, I guess. Final smoothing out. The poor guys will be walking in their sleep tonight. But it's his play, isn't it?" That, Shapiro supposed, did not require an answer. He thanked Mrs. Abel, who said, "Is there something important you want to see him about?

"Just routine," Shapiro told her, and thanked her again for her help and went out of the booth. Tony Cook was waiting for him at the desk. They went a few steps away from it, toward the hotel's entrance.

"No atropine in the medicine cabinet," Tony said. "Didn't suppose there would be, did we? Bufferin. Nembutal, fifty mg, one or two capsules at bedtime and needed for sleep. Doctor: A.

T. Perrine. Bottle of eye drops. Prescription; both eyes, three times daily, every four hours. Not the same doctor. Carl Jenkins, M.D., this one is, address on Park."

"And no atropine sulfate, Tony? Could be it's dispensed under a trade name, of course. The way Nembutal's a trade name for one of the barbiturates."

"Just Bufferin, Nembutal and these eye drops," Tony told him.

"Wouldn't leave the stuff around in plain sight if he's been feeding it to Askew," Shapiro said.

They went out onto Forty-fourth Street and walked toward the Rolf Simon Theater.

12

The lobby of the Rolf Simon Theater was almost deserted. Four women and two men formed a small cluster near the box office, which was unoccupied. A sign explained why: OPEN 10 A.M.

It still lacked ten minutes of that hour.

Shapiro and Cook found the doors leading into the auditorium locked against them. But as Tony tried one of them for the second time, it clicked at him and opened. Now there was a man in the box office and the ticket window was open. The box-office man smiled and nodded at them in—Nathan assumed—welcome. At any rate, he had evidently pressed a button which released a lock.

They went into the theater. The stage was lighted, and Price and Arlene Collins were on it, both dressed for tennis. And both, in tennis shorts, very good-looking. Price was definitely the older, but not, in appearance, too much the older. Forty to the girl's early twenties—about right, from what Nathan had read of the play. The clothes Price wore so well, the movements he now made so smoothly, might have been difficult for a man in his sixties. For, say, Clive Branson.

"At love, my dear," Price said to the pretty young woman who was his wife in *Summer Solstice.* "On court—"

"Now you've got it, Ken," Robert Kirby, the director, said from his aisle seat. "Obvious, and he knows it's obvious. That's

111

got to show in the reading. The way you want it, Bret?"

"He's got it," Bret Askew said from the seat beside Kirby.

"Only he'll have to pitch it up a bit," Rolf Simon said from a seat in the last row of the orchestra. "Blurry from here."

"All right from up here, R.S." The voice was young and female and came, evidently, from the balcony. "You in that dead spot?"

"Yes, I guess so. Thing is, there'll be customers in it. Tonight, we hope. All right. Take a break. Then we'll do Act Three from the top. We've got visitors at the moment. Those guardians of the law again." Rolf Simon stood up, tall and burly, and came across toward the men from Homicide. When he was a little way from them, he said, "Seeing quite a good deal of you two, aren't we?" His tone was flat. There was no pleasure in his heavy voice.

"Sorry, Mr. Simon," Shapiro said. "Happens to be our job."

"And ours is getting a play ready for tonight. For eight fifteen tonight, so McClay from the *Chronicle* can make an edition. If he decides to come at all. The *Sentinel* dame says she can't make it. She'll try to drop in in a day or two. So—what're you after, Lieutenant?"

"Just a few words with Mr. Price. And with you too, Mr. Simon. During the break."

"O.K." Again there was no pleasure in Rolf Simon's voice. He raised it. "Stretch the break out," he said. "Make it for coffee. And, Price, the cops want to talk to you." Then, to Shapiro and Cook, "I'll go upstairs for my coffee. Come up when you're through with Price. And I hope to God you don't upset him; he's jittery enough as it is. But doing O.K., I'll say that for him. See you." With that he went out into the lobby.

Kenneth Price came down from the stage. On his way up the aisle, he stopped by the fourth-row seat in which Bret Askew was sitting next to the director, leaned down, and said something to Askew.

Cook and Shapiro could not hear what he said, but they could hear Askew's answer: "Sure." He got up, and the two came up the aisle together.

Askew said, "Morning, Lieutenant. Look, I was going to try to get you on the phone."

Shapiro said, "Yes?"

"Thing is," Askew said, "I guess I made a fool of myself last night. With Detective Cook here. About—well, somebody trying to poison me. Putting this alkaloid in my drink. Probably wasn't anything in the drink. Except—all right—alcohol. What I'm trying to say is, maybe I had one or two too many. If you see what I mean. O.K.?"

"If you say so, Mr. Askew. Tony?"

"This doctor the hotel sent up," Tony said. "He agreed the symptoms were those of mild poisoning by one of the belladonna group. Atropine sulfate, he thought."

"Afraid I sold him a bill of goods," Askew said, "not meaning to, actually. Thing is, I was—call it fantasizing. Part of my trade, you could say. Few years back, I looked up the alkaloids; thought of using atropine poisoning in a play. I never did, actually. But the notion sort of stuck in my mind, I suppose. And—well, I acted it out. Make sense to you, Shapiro?"

It didn't, particularly. Shapiro's "Mmm" was noncommittal.

"Tempest in a teacup, really," Askew said. "Or a cocktail glass. And I'm damn sorry. Got a little spiffed and—well, fed you and Cook here herring. Damn childish thing to do, I'll admit that. O.K.?"

For a moment nobody said anything. The silence was Tony Cook's cue. "Well," Tony said, "you sure fooled me, Mr. Askew. Fooled the doctor, too. And—it was all just a game?

113

Only—well, how'd you get your pupils to dilate? The pupils of your eyes, that is."

Price had sat down in an aisle seat, his attitude that of a mildly interested bystander. Now he spoke. "Wouldn't alcohol account for that, Mr. Cook?"

"I don't really know," Tony said. "Have to ask a doctor about that, wouldn't we? But—we did last night, didn't we, Mr. Askew? And he thought mild alkaloid poisoning.. Just because you suggested it, you think? Only he did want you to go to a hospital for tests, didn't he? Make himself look pretty silly, wouldn't he, if he'd sent a mildly drunk man to be tested for alkaloid poisoning?"

"There's that," Shapiro said. "There is that, Mr. Askew. You're pretty sure, now, that you were just mildly intoxicated?"

Askew merely nodded. Shapiro said, "Yes, Mr. Price?" Kenneth Price merely looked at him. "Sorry," Shapiro said. "I thought you were about to say something."

"Just," Price said, "that we only had a couple of drinks each. Not doubles or anything like that."

"Could be," Askew said, "I had a couple while I was waiting for you."

"O.K., Bret," Price said. "Though you seemed sober enough to me when we were talking about my readings. But have it your way."

"Sure," Askew said. "I thought I was—sober enough, that is. Sort of crept up on me, maybe. Up so tight about the play these days. When I relaxed, I relaxed too much, maybe. Plays are hell."

Shapiro raised dark eyebrows.

"Writing plays for a living," Askew said. "A tense trade, Lieutenant. Will it jell? Will anybody produce it? Will the director and the actors get what you're driving at? And what about

114

the critics? Will people come? There's no business like show business, as Berlin said. Tension all the time. Right, Ken?"

"Goes for actors too," Price said. "You end up tense as hell."

He did not look particularly tense at the moment, Shapiro thought, for all he was to take over a starring role that evening. He looked—well, contented was probably the word for Kenneth Price. The look he had was of a man whose big chance has landed in his lap. Or, of course, has been pushed there.

"Mr. Askew called you yesterday afternoon and asked you to come down and have a drink with him, to talk over the readings he wanted in the play. That's the way it was, Mr. Price?"

"Yes. Certain lines he wanted a special twist on."

Shapiro said he saw. "Way I get it, the two of you sat at a table near the entrance to the restaurant. People would pass close to your table on their way into the restaurant?"

"Sure. A lot did."

"Anyone you knew? Any members of the cast, say?"

"A couple of guys I knew. Not connected with *Summer Solstice,* if that's what you're getting at."

"And someone could have dropped something in your glass, or Mr. Askew's glass, without being noticed?"

Price supposed so. "We were pretty much taken up with what we were talking about. Trying to get the readings Bret wanted. Engrossed, I guess you could call it."

"Listen, Lieutenant—" Askew said.

Shapiro cut in. "Yes, Mr. Askew," he said. "I know you don't think now that anything was put in your drink. We just have to cover everything, you see. All possibilities. Mr. Price?"

"Yes?"

"Nobody stopped by the table last night—to say hello?"

"Only my agent. Mrs. Abel, you know. Just as Bret and I were finishing up, actually. You see—well, I was going over to

115

her place for dinner. To talk some things over. Her office is a few blocks from the Algonquin and her chauffeur picks her up in the evenings. She thought she might as well stop by and pick me up too. Save me cab fare, was the way she put it."

"Knowing you'd be in the lobby having a drink with Mr. Askew?"

"Yes. I'd given her a ring telling her I'd be with Bret."

"And she came in herself? Didn't send in this chauffeur of hers?"

"Yes. Wanted to say hello to Bret, here, and, I suppose, see how we were making out. After all, she's my agent. Wants to keep up with things. Particularly now, when things are, you could say, a little shaky. If you know that I mean."

"Yes," Shapiro said. "But I gather they're firming up."

"They seem to be, Lieutenant. We'll know after tonight. Know better, anyway."

"Anything you want to ask these gentlemen, Cook?" Shapiro said. "Anything you feel we've missed?"

"No, sir. Seem to have covered everything. Only—well, last night, when I still thought somebody had tried to poison Mr. Askew, I had a crazy notion. Seems crazy now, anyway."

"Yes, Cook?"

"That somebody was really after the play. Knock off the star. Feed the playwright something that'd make him sick. Idea, to stop the play. Close it down and make sure it couldn't be put back together again."

"And why the hell would anybody want to do that?" Askew said.

"I know it's a crazy notion," Tony told him. "Said it was. I don't know anything about writing plays, Mr. Askew. Writing anything, for that matter. But I thought, you know, perhaps authors draw their characters from real life. And that maybe one of

116

the characters in *Summer Solstice* could be identified as a real person. And that somebody, the person himself or someone close to him, objected to that. Another crazy notion, I suppose."

"It sure as hell is," Askew said. "No, Cook, there's no prototype for any of the characters in my play. Not the way I write."

"But some authors do, don't they?"

"A few. Not very many, I'd think. Oh, Somerset Maugham did now and then. In *Cakes and Ale*, for example. There've been other cases. And sure, fictional characters, in novels or plays, have to come from somewhere. From everybody the author has ever met, including himself. But there's nobody in *Summer Solstice* who's taken from real life. Nobody at all. So, nobody to resent the play. Not for that reason, anyway. It doesn't libel anyone."

"All right," Tony said. "It was a crazy idea. As I admitted."

"So," Shapiro said, "we've got that cleared up. I think we'll have a word or two with Mr. Simon. Don't you, Cook?"

When it is "Cook" instead of "Tony," formality is indicated, so Tony said, "Sir." And Kenneth Price said, "I'm going to round up that coffee. And then we'll have to get on with it, won't we, Bret?"

The playwright and the actor went back down the aisle toward the stage. Shapiro and Cook watched them go. Then the two from Homicide South went out into the lobby. There was a short line in front of the box-office window. Nathan and Tony went to the narrow door to Rolf Simon's elevator; the door was closed and locked. Shapiro lifted a hand toward the man in the box office, who saluted in return and nodded. He pressed something and the door lock clicked. Tony opened the door and they went into the narrow elevator. Tony pressed the button marked UP and up they went.

"All the same," Tony said, "his eyes looked funny. Damn

funny. The way they do after an eye doctor has put drops in them."

"Yes," Shapiro said, "I guess they did, Tony."

"And so Askew's covering for somebody? Price?"

"Could be. Way it looks, isn't it? Or maybe Mrs. Abel, of course. Or—God knows."

The elevator stopped, and they went into Simon's somewhat elegant office. It was empty, but the door beyond was open, and Simon's heavy voice came through it. "Back here, gentlemen," Simon said.

They went back there, into Rolf Simon's living room.

The producer was sitting on a sofa in front of a glass-topped coffee table. There was a silver tray on the table and on it a silver coffeepot and two cups and also a cream pitcher which matched the pot. There were two comfortable-looking chairs on the opposite side of the coffee table.

"Sit down," Simon said. "Have some coffee."

They sat. They accepted coffee—very good coffee. Urged, Shapiro added cream to his. Tony took his black.

"Now," Simon said, "our playwright says nobody tried to poison him; he just had one too many. That what he told you two?"

It was what Askew had told them.

"Believe him?"

Shapiro answered with a standard "Mmm."

"At least," Simon said, "you're not going to arrest Ken Price. Which would be damned inconvenient. He's shaping up well for the part. Anyway, why would he try to knock off Askew? Because Askew saw him putting poison in Clive Branson's drink?"

"From what Mr. Askew says now, nobody tried to kill him. Or even make him sick. But yes. That could have been a motive. For somebody."

"And with old Clive dead," Simon said, "Ken gets a fat part.

Starring, you could call it. Leading man, anyway. More press and more money. The Abel will see to that. Doing her damnedest right now. And wants run of the play."

"Which, as I understand it, Branson had," Nathan said.

"He did," Simon said. "Box office, Branson was."

"Why did you engage him for the part, Mr. Simon?" It was Tony who asked this, keeping his tone entirely casual.

"That entered in. And Branson was one hell of an actor."

"Was," Shapiro said, "or had been, Mr. Simon?"

Simon drained his coffee cup and then refilled it. Then he spoke, his heavy voice low. He said, "Been reading the notices, Lieutenant?" He paused. "No, I heard it from Askew. Ever hear Percy Hammond's line, either of you? 'The more you praise an actor, the less it likes you.' Marking the 'it' *stet* for the proofreader."

Both Shapiro and Cook shook their heads.

"A critic, Hammond was. On the old *Tribune*. Gone now, the paper is. So is Percy. He was good; made sense a lot of the time. More than you can say for critics nowadays. Where were we?"

"Talking about Branson," Shapiro said, "and why you hired him to play the lead in *Summer Solstice*. Just because he was a box-office draw, Mr. Simon?"

"Askew wanted him," Simon said. "Held out for him, if we could get him. And I like to keep my playwrights happy, when it's possible. Isn't, very often. Cranky breed, playwrights."

"Askew wanted Mr. Branson a great deal?"

"Authors want the world. In the old days they wanted all three Barrymores, both Lunts, and Cornell to boot. But Askew did have a point. Man like Branson, with a reputation like his, does bring in the customers. And, O.K., the investors. Backers. Not that a lot of the money in *Summer Solstice* isn't mine. Most of it, actually. But—well, it costs one hell of a lot to bring a play

119

in nowadays. Even a one-setter like *Solstice*. In the old days you could do it for peanuts. Not that it felt like peanuts then. But with orchestra seats going at three thirty—for straight plays, that is—we could still get by. With luck and decent reviews in the *Times* and the *Herald-Tribune* and maybe the *Sun* and the *Post*—well, we didn't starve. It's different, now. People stay home and watch TV. Don't even go to movies the way they used to. And—" He broke off and shrugged heavy shoulders. "Not what you came here to get," he said. "Laments for the good old days. What do you want, Lieutenant? Mr. Cook?"

"Were you upset by the reviews of *Solstice*? The suggestion that Branson was too old for the part?"

Simon lighted a cigarette before he answered. Then he said, "Think I need a couple of scribblers to tell me my business? Hell, it showed up in the first rehearsal. First read-through, actually. But by then we were stuck with him. Not that he was bad, you understand. Old Clive was a pro. Only—tell you the truth—he wasn't too damn good, either. We kept hoping he'd work into it. Probably the old boy hoped so too. This is between us, gentlemen?"

"If possible," Shapiro said. "If it hasn't anything to do with Mr. Branson's death."

"Trouble with me is, I talk too damned much," Simon said. "But what, for Christ's sake, could his being too old for the part have to do with his being bumped off? If he was. Are you sure he was, Shapiro?"

"If somebody who knew of his lack of tolerance for barbiturates put one of them in his drink, we're sure enough," Shapiro said. "Sure enough to go on poking around. Eventually, it's up to the District Attorney, of course."

"You say you were stuck with him, Mr. Simon," Tony said. "Couldn't you just—well, ease him out? Fire him, I mean."

120

"You don't just fire a man like Branson, Cook. A star, with his name above the title of the play. There's Equity, for one thing. Also, there's a contract. A damn good one, from his point of view. Run of the play, he held out for. Or the Abel dame did for him. Run of the play or no Clive Branson. And we wanted him. The backers wanted him. And the customers wanted him. Seen him in movies. Heard about him. You don't just fire a star like that, Cook. Maybe you try to buy him off. Buy up his contract."

Simon sighed. He crushed his cigarette out in a glass ashtray.

"A run-of-the-play contract is hard to buy up. You say—Oh, six months maybe. The actor says six years. Maybe ten years. Hell, maybe forever. Worse when we used to send out touring companies. Oh, all right, I had a stab at it; made him a decent offer. Thought for a while he might take it. Reasonable guy, as actors go. But not the Abel girl. She's a tough one. Trying now to get run of the play for Price. She knows better than to try to hold me up for what I was paying Branson. But she wants plenty. *And* a cut of the profits. Jesus!"

"Which, I take it, she's not going to get?" Shapiro said.

"Nothing like what she wants for him," Simon said. "But— well, a hell of a lot. We've got that damn good advance sale. Don't know how much of it will cancel out, as I told you before. After those reviews. But with Clive out of the picture, who knows? No rush for refunds has showed up yet, anyway. So. The Abel's in a pretty good position. I've a hell of a lot of money tied up in the show. Devil and the deep blue sea. And she's the dame to know it."

"The way it sounds," Shapiro said, "Price stands to profit from Branson's death. Financially and, I suppose, professionally."

"You can say that," Simon said. "If it goes all right tonight.

121

But, hell, enough to kill for? If that's what you're getting at, Lieutenant. For all he knew, I could have decided to close the show. Or look around for another big-timer to take over the part. Ken Price doesn't have any stranglehold on it, even yet, and *knows* he hasn't. All right, maybe he gains. But what a damn long chance for him to take, wouldn't it be? I don't figure Price to be that kind of a damn fool."

"Can you think of anyone else who benefits, Mr. Simon?"

"If things work out right, I do," Simon said. "Save a lot on what I was paying Branson—if they keep coming."

"Anyone else?"

"Branson's been making a lot of jack in Hollywood. For several years. May have held on to a good deal of it. Which will go to somebody now, I suppose."

"Had he any relatives you know of? Anyone who would inherit?"

Simon did not know. Branson had been married several times. "He was a great one for marrying them. A good many of the Hollywood boys are. Particularly the older ones. Looks better to the public, I suppose they think."

"All his marriages ended in divorce?"

Simon supposed so.

"Did he have a lawyer, that you know of?"

Simon sure as hell knew that. So much haggling over the contract, first the Abel dame's lawyer, then Branson's. "Mine too, for God's sake—wasted a hell of a lot of time on it, for my money. And for my money it sure as hell was. Man named Fisk, Branson's mouthpiece was. Morton Fisk. You're wondering about a will?"

"Yes. And whether all his marriages did end in divorces. Legally, he may still have been a resident of California."

"Yes," Simon said. "Community property. One of his former

122

wives is in the cast, you know. Cast of *Solstice*. Plays the mother. Nice actress. Nice girl, for that matter."

"We knew that, yes. From a friend of Detective Cook's in fact. Barnes, isn't it?"

"Helen. Yes."

"Any tension between them that you know of?"

There had not been. "They were friendly enough. Friction I'd have spotted, or Kirby would have. Couldn't have had that sort of thing messing the performance up, could we? Would have had to let her go, I suppose. But they got along all right. Friendly as anything. Why not? She was several wives back, way I got it."

Nathan Shapiro, and then Tony Cook, stood up to go.

Simon also got up. For a heavy man, he moved easily and well. "I'll go down with you," he said. "See how they're getting on with it."

The elevator would just hold the three of them. On the lobby floor, Simon went into the auditorium. He said, "Probably be seeing you," as he went in.

Shapiro and Cook went out to the street. On the marquee, there were two men on ladders. They were taking light bulbs out of the sign which read CLIVE BRANSON. It had been above **"Summer Solstice,** a new comedy by BRET ASKEW." Askew's name was in much smaller lettering than the name of the star had been.

13

They found telephone booths, complete with Manhattan directories. Nathan found "Fisk Morton atty," with an office on West Fortieth. Tony found the office addresses of the two doctors who had written prescriptions for Kenneth Price. Not that either was likely to be forthcoming about a patient, he reminded Nathan Shapiro. They would meet somewhere for lunch?

"Oh, all right, Tony. The Algonquin would be convenient." It would also be expensive.

In the lobby of the West Fortieth building, the directory listed Fisk, Latham and Cohen, Attorneys. The law offices were on the sixth floor. Nathan went up to the sixth floor. A dignified, rather matronly woman in the outer office asked if she could help him. Did he have an appointment? Well . . . Mr. Fisk was with a client. If Lieutenant—Shapiro, was it?—would wait a few minutes, she would tell Mr. Fisk that—"Oh, Mr. Snyder," to a middle-aged man who came through a door from an inner office. Mr. Snyder said, "Uh," and went out of the law offices of Fisk, Latham and Cohen. The matronly receptionist picked up the telephone on her desk and pressed a button in its base.

"There is a police lieutenant here who would like a few minutes of your time, sir. . . . No, sir, he didn't say. I'll ask him."

"About Clive Branson's will," Shapiro told her. "Entirely a routine matter."

She relayed the information. She cradled the telephone.

124

"Right through there, Lieutenant. At the end of the corridor."

Morton Fisk's office was large, with windows through which one could see Bryant Park and the Public Library. Fisk sat at a desk with his back to the windows. It was a large desk with nothing on its top. And Morton Fisk was a large man, probably in his forties. He looked at Shapiro across the desk and said, "Yes?"

A rountine matter, Shapiro said again. Concerning his late client, Clive Branson, the actor, whose sudden death the police were looking into. The contents of his will might, conceivably, help in the investigation.

"Matter of fact," Fisk said, "I've rather been expecting you, from the coy way the newspapers handled the story. You people really think somebody killed the old boy?"

"We think it possible, Mr. Fisk."

Fisk opened the top drawer of his desk and took a blue-bound document out of it. He put it on his desk and pushed it toward Shapiro. He said, "Sit down, Lieutenant."

Nathan sat.

"Filing it for probate this afternoon," Fisk said. "Read it, if you want to. Or I'll give you the gist." Fisk did not wait to be answered. "Fifty thousand each to his three surviving ex-wives," Fisk said. "He had four, you know. One, an English one, died a few years back. Cynthia Desmond—sounds like a stage name, doesn't it?—Carol Franklin, Helen Barnes, Felicia Leonard. She was the one who died. Residue to Edgar Lord, 'for long service.' "

"That's all of it, Mr. Fisk?"

"Yes. Oh, 'In memory of happy days' in each bequest to an ex."

"Any idea what Lord will get? After the hundred and fifty is paid?"

"No. I was Branson's lawyer, not his business manager. Chap

125

named Parnell handled his financial affairs. I gather he had plenty. If the contract he had with Rolf Simon was at all typical, he damn well must have had. Ten thousand a week for run of the play. And a lot from the movies. Percentage of the gross on the last two. One of them went over big, I happen to know. The last one—well, not so great, they tell me."

"Of the four wives—all divorced, I take it—where does Helen Barnes fit in? In the—er, sequence?"

"Next to last. The Franklin girl was the last. And the youngest. Working in Hollywood now. Yes, they all got divorces. All by mutual consent. With the best of feelings on both sides. Oh, we had to rig the Barker one. In New York, that was. In the old days. When it had to be adultery, you know."

"Miss Barnes is in the play Branson was starring in," Shapiro said.

Fisk knew that. He also knew Helen Barnes. "Nice woman—younger than Branson, probably. Early forties would be my guess. Doesn't look even that. Makeup woman must have to age her some for the mother role."

"You've seen the play, Mr. Fisk?"

"Just read the reviews. Heard one on TV. Not so kind to Branson, that one was. Or, too damn kind, if you get what I mean. Too old for the part, although it grieves me to say so. Damning with faint praise, to use the cliché. Look, Lieutenant don't get any ideas about Helen Barnes just because of the fifty thousand. She's a damn nice person. Any wild ideas, I mean."

"I try not to get wild ideas, Mr. Fisk. But I will have to have a word with Miss Barnes, won't I? Does she know about this bequest?"

"Not from me. Of course, Branson may have told her. Chances are he did."

"Yes," Shapiro said, and stood up. He thanked the attorney for his help.

Fisk hoped he had helped. He said that old Clive was one hell of a nice guy, and that he wished Shapiro all the luck in the world in finding whoever had knocked him off. If, in fact, somebody had.

Shapiro walked through Bryant Park on his way to the Rolf Simon Theater. The rain had let up, but it was a chilly late morning. People sitting on the Bryant Park benches wrapped coats and raincoats around them.

So Helen Barnes was a damn nice person. To Morton Fisk, at any rate. To Rolf Simon, too. But murderers can be nice persons, to friends if not to victims. It seemed probable to Shapiro that Miss Barnes had known she was fifty thousand dollars richer because of Branson's death. It seemed certain that as his wife, she had known of his intolerance to barbiturates.

There was a flat-bottom truck parked in front of the Rolf Simon Theater, and a patrolman was guiding traffic around it. Several men were easing down from the marquee and loading onto the truck a large, ungainly structure. It was the sign reading CLIVE BRANSON IN from which, an hour or so before, two men had been removing light bulbs. What was left, complete with bulbs that were lighted, was **Summer Solstice,** a new comedy by BRET ASKEW. So. Shapiro waited until CLIVE BRANSON was safely stowed and went into the theater lobby. There was no one in the lobby. The box-office window was lowered. There was a sign on the ledge in front of the window: TONIGHT'S PERFORMANCE SOLD OUT. One of the doors into the auditorium was unlocked. Nathan went in.

Robert Kirby, the director, was in the fourth-row, center-aisle seat. Bret Askew was in the seat beside him. In the darkened auditorium, Shapiro could not see the heavy figure of Rolf Simon. He stood for a minute and looked down toward the lighted stage. Then he saw Simon. He was in a seat well back and on a side aisle.

There were two women on the stage, both watching two men leaving the set's living room for the set's terrace—a terrace bright with sunlight. One of the men was Kenneth Price; the other, slighter and younger, was the newly selected man in what, clearly, was the play's triangle. Both were dressed for tennis and carried rackets.

The women watching them were Arlene Collins, playing the twenty-year-old wife, and Helen Barnes, playing her mother. "And may the best man—" Helen Barnes said, and the director spoke from his seat. "Hit the irony a little harder, Barnes," he said. Helen Barnes, who looked just barely old enough for a mother's role, repeated her line. It sounded much the same to Nathan, but Kirby said, "That's it, darling. You know damn well who's going to win. So does the audience." And then, his voice a little more raised, "O.K., we'll break for lunch. Make it—oh, about one thirty. Right?"

Price came back into the forestage. He said, "You'll have us all hoarse for tonight, Bob. Nobody'll be able to hear any of us—beyond the first row, anyway."

"A couple of hours will do it," Kirby said. "The second-act curtain still needs a little smoothing." He got up and came up the aisle.

Askew came behind him. "My God, you again," Askew said.

"Yes," Shapiro said. "But not long this time, Mr. Askew. Just want a word or two with Miss Barnes."

"She'll be in her dressing room, probably," Kirby said. "Room Three. One flight up, You can go across the stage if you want to."

Shapiro went down the aisle and climbed the fragile steps and crossed the impromptu bridge to the stage. He left it by way of the lighted terrace. It wasn't as real as it had looked from the orchestra. The vista of green land beyond it turned out to be paint-

128

ed on canvas. Shapiro turned to his right. After a few yards the terrace ended. A wall stopped him, and he turned right again and walked beside canvas nailed to wooden framework. LR WALL, L was lettered on one panel of the structure. Of course—the flat which, on the other side, was a wall of the living room of the Derwent house on Long Island.

He came to a flight of stairs. A man in work clothes was sitting on the bottom step. "Dressing room up there?" Shapiro asked.

"Some of them, Mac. Want to visit somebody?"

Shapiro told the man whom he wanted to visit.

"Yeah," the man said. "Kid from the deli just took her lunch up."

He stood up and gestured Shapiro toward the stairs. Shapiro climbed them. At the top there was a corridor, with doors on either side of it. The door on his right had the numeral 3 painted on it. It was closed. Shapiro knocked. "Yes?" came in a female voice from the other side of the door.

"Miss Barnes?"

"Who else?"

"Lieutenant Shapiro," Nathan said. (Would the "Lieutenant" ever stop sticking in his throat?) "Could I see you for a couple of minutes?"

"Oh," he heard, "the policeman. Come on in, if you want to. "I'm decent."

He went in. Helen Barnes was sitting at a dressing table, eating a sandwich and, apparently, drinking a Coke. Her back was to Shapiro. The room contained, in addition to the dressing table, a couch and an upholstered chair. Helen's back was a young back, and slender. She turned to face Shapiro as he went in. Her face, too, was a young face. Styles change, Nathan thought; he could remember when the mother of a woman of twenty would be played by an actress apparently in her fifties and not making out very well.

He told Helen Barnes again who he was.

She said, "I know, Lieutenant. By now, everybody knows. Yes, I was at the party. No, I didn't put poison in Clive's drink. Also, I don't know who did." She drank her Coke. She said, "He was a really nice man."

"And," Shapiro said, "an ex-husband of yours, Miss Barnes."

"Of course," she said. "Everybody knows that. Ex as of four years ago next month. All very friendly, it was."

"And you had been married how long, Miss Barnes? It is Miss, I take it?"

"Or M.S., pronounced 'Miz.'" Which is the way they pronounced 'Mrs.' where I grew up. In Missouri, that was—pronounced "mizzooruh,' by the way. Clive and I had been married about two years when we decided it wasn't working out."

"Long enough," Shapiro said, "to learn he couldn't tolerate barbiturates."

"Yes, Lieutenant, oh, yes. Was that how it was done?" She frowned. "A sneaky way of going about it, seems to me. Yes, I knew Clive couldn't take the stuff. And, yes, I can. And do, fifty mgs at bedtime for sleep. And another fifty half an hour later, if still awake. Which mostly I'm not. But I didn't drop a capsule in Clive's drink, and I didn't see anybody else do it, either." She took another sip from her Coke. "Of course," she said, "you don't have to believe me, do you?"

Shapiro didn't answer the question, if it was a question. Instead, he said, "Did you know Mr. Branson had left you money in his will, Miss Barnes?"

"Yes," she said. "Sweet of him. But he was sweet. And no, he didn't mention any amount to me."

"A sizable sum," Shapiro said. "At least to me. Fifty thousand each to you and the two other surviving former wives."

"Neither of whom was around to put sleeping medicine in Clive's drink," she said. "Leaving me on the limb. All by myself?"

The last was a question. Shapiro answered it with a shake of his head.

"Then," Helen Barnes said, "I'll have time to finish my sandwich. Bacon and tomato on toasted white, Lieutenant, and I've actually got a spare if you'd like it."

Shapiro thanked her and declined the offer. He found his way out of the Rolf Simon Theater and walked to the Algonquin.

Tony Cook was already in the lobby, which was beginning to fill with pre-lunch drinkers. Tony had a table for two, with a glass on it. Bourbon on the rocks, Nathan assumed, knowing Tony's noontime habits. Nathan sat down and rang the little bell. Tony raised inquiring eyebrows.

"Helen Barnes—she plays the mother in *Solstice*—" Nathan told him, "used to be married to Branson. A few years back. Divorce very amiable, she says. Association in the play, likewise. He left her fifty thousand in his will. Left two other previous wives the same."

"And, being married to him, she'd be likely, be almost certain to know he couldn't tolerate Nembutal, or whatever it was. And she was at the party."

He said the last with a rising inflection.

"No," Shapiro said, "I'm afraid not. Doesn't seem the type— not to me, anyway. All very open about everything. Yes, she'd known about a bequest, and of course she knew Branson was oversensitive to barbiturates. And would I like a bacon and tomato sandwich? She had a spare. They'd taken a lunch break, and she was having hers in her dressing room. Very open and aboveboard, the lady seems to be."

131

It was unlike Nate to be so favorably impressed by personalities, to brush off suspicion so easily. Helen Barnes, whom Tony remembered only vaguely having seen on the *Solstice* stage, must be, off it, a very convincing woman.

"How about you?" Nathan said, and then, to a waiter, "A sherry, please. Not too dry." Not that the stipulation would get him much of anywhere. The Algonquin does not serve sweet sherry as a pre-lunch aperitif.

"Dr. Jenkins is an eye man," Tony said. "Ophthalmologist. Rather forthcoming, as doctors go. Price is subject to attacks of glaucoma, the painful type. Acute narrow-angle, he called it. Under treatment, and coming along quite well. What the eye drops are for, Jenkins says. Only thing he's prescribed for Price. This other doctor, Perrine, is on vacation, it turns out. He's an internist. May very well have prescribed a barbiturate for Price, Jenkins said. Nothing unusual about that."

"Did you prescribe atropine for Price, Doctor?" Tony had asked Jenkins. "Or any of the belladonna group of alkaloids?"

Jenkins certainly had not. Highly contraindicated for people with Price's type of glaucoma. Might well bring on an attack.

Would Dr. Perrine be likely to have prescribed such medication?

"He knows about Price's glaucoma," Jenkins said. "Told him myself. We physicians do exchange information about a patient we both have. To prevent just that sort of cross-up—prescribing a belladonna alkaloid in a case like Price's"

And, Tony told Nathan, after the waiter had brought the sherry (which was dry), a belladonna alkaloid like atropine wasn't, certainly wasn't, something you could simply ask for at the corner drugstore. Not ask for and get.

As for prescribing atropine, Tony was told that he was not distinguishing between giving it systemically and giving it topi-

132

cally. Which meant, it turned out, whether it was to be taken internally or used externally— like eye drops or ointment. For example, Dr. Jenkins said, he routinely prescribed drops containing atropine following cataract surgery. "But it's quite a while since I've had anything to do with the gut," he had added. "Keeping up with the eyes is all I have time for."

Had Dr. Jenkins any idea what one of the belladonna alkaloids would be prescribed for—um, systemically?

Of course he did. Spastic or irritable colon. Perhaps acute enterocolitis. Perhaps peptic ulcer. Dosage small: fraction of an mg, probably several times a day.

"Doesn't get us much of anywhere," Shapiro said, and took a sip of his sherry. Sour, as he had expected. Tony agreed that his talk with Dr. Jenkins hadn't got them anywhere. If Price had had atropine to drop into Askew's drink, he hadn't got it from Jenkins. Or, presumably, from Dr. Perrine, who wouldn't be back from vacation for another ten days. So?

"Mr. Simon seems to have given this surprise party for Branson," Shapiro said. "Provided the food and drink. And the service too, wouldn't you think? A bartender and a waiter. Perhaps somebody to cook. Outside people, with outside points of view. Maybe one of them noticed something. Wonder who they were, don't you, Tony? Oh, finish your drink."

Tony Cook did, in a gulp. He went across the lobby and into a phone booth. He stayed for several minutes.

"Greenwich Catering Service," he told Shapiro. "Simon's secretary set it up. Says Mr. Simon uses them now and then. Finds them very reliable. And they're in the phone book."

"Greenwich?" Shapiro said.

"For Greenwich Avenue," Tony told him. "In the Village. Shall we . . . ?"

They might as well have lunch first, now that they were there.

133

Shapiro finished his sour sherry—"*dry*," for God's sake!—and they went into the restaurant. Nathan had broiled scrod; Tony, chicken potpie. Both were very good. They did not hurry over lunch. After they had finished, they walked to Sixth Avenue and took the Sixth Avenue subway downtown to the West Fourth Street station.

The Greenwich Avenue address Tony had got from the Manhattan telephone directory was that of a four-story building with a restaurant on the ground floor. The Greenwich Catering Service was on the third. They climbed stairs to get to it. It was a not-very-large room with two people in it, one male and one female. They were both at desks, and the woman, youngish and reasonably attractive, was on the telephone. The man was writing something down on a memo pad. He looked up and said, "Yes?"

Shapiro told him who they were and what they wanted. The man said, "Mr. Simon's party Sunday night. That would be Sam and Otto, wouldn't it, Ruth?"

The woman said, "Six thirty then, Mrs. Bell, and white jacket." She cradled the telephone and said, "Yes, Mr. Owen. Sam and Otto. Sam's due to check in. Otto's at the Smirnoffs', you know. Do these . . ."

"Policemen," Shapiro said as she hesitated.

". . . want to see both of them?"

One would do, Shapiro told her. For the moment, anyway.

"Sam ought to call in about now," Owen said. "See if we've got anything for him. He—" The phone rang on his desk. He said, "Yes?" into it and then, "Oh, Sam. Couple of cops here want to see you. About the party Mr. Simon gave. . . . Yeah, for the actor. . . . Yeah, the dead one. . . . No, nobody thinks you did. Come along in, huh?"

134

He hung up.

"He'll be right along," he said. "Lives just around the corner, sort of. Says he didn't bump anybody off. You heard what I told him. Hope I was right. Good bartender, Sam is. Anyway, we don't get many squawks about him. And we've got a job for him tonight."

"He'll be available," Shapiro said. "Far's I know, anyway. We'll wait for him."

They did not have to wait long: a little less than ten minutes. Sam—Sam Scanlon, as it turned out—was a stocky man, probably in his fifties. He had an affable face, appropriate to a bartender.

Yes, he and Otto had served Mr. Simon's party at Mr. Branson's house. It was Branson, wasn't it? An actor, he understood. Never heard of him, himself. Otto had. Said he was a star in the movies. The party? Just a party. He made drinks, Scotch or bourbon and water, mostly. Poured champagne for those who wanted it. Yes, he and Otto had supplied the liquor. And the sandwiches and cheese things. Yes, sometimes the firm supplied the drinks and food, although usually the customer did. But this had been a surprise party, way he got it. This Mr. Branson hadn't known people were coming. No way of knowing whether he'd have drinks and food—well, just lying around. Anyway, the party was on Mr. Simon, wasn't it?

He and Otto had showed up around nine thirty, as ordered. Mr. Branson's man had let them in. Yes, he seemed to have expected them. Not all that much a surprise to him, way it looked. The man—butler? Well, he looked like a butler. Not that Sam had met many butlers. "People who have them don't usually have us in, do they?—oh, dresser." Anyway, the man had taken them to the kitchen of the house, and they'd got the ice cubes out

135

and put the champagne on ice, and put on their jackets. White jackets, not tuxedos. As Mr. Owen had directed. Right, Mr. Owen?

People had started coming around ten. Mr. Branson's man had let them in. Oh, ten or eleven of them, he thought. All there by, say, ten thirty. All, way he got it, connected with a play Mr. Simon was putting on. That was Mr. Simon's line, putting on plays. The guests at the party had moved around a good deal. It was a big room with plenty of places to sit. Yes, when they moved around they usually carried their drinks with them. Well, no, not always. Sometimes they left them on the tables they'd been sitting near. Yes, if people didn't come back to their drinks, he'd pick them up, or Otto would, and they'd rinse the glasses off ready for fresh drinks as wanted. But more often than not, the people would come back to where they'd left their glasses and finish what was in them. Oh, yes, twice, he thought, people got their glasses mixed up. One time, he remembered, one of the women had picked up a glass from one of the tables and said, "But this is *bourbon!* Who stole my Scotch?" Like it was a joke.

"By the way," Shapiro said, "do you happen to remember what Mr. Branson was drinking?"

"I sure do. Scotch and a little water and no ice. Very strong on the no-ice bit, he was."

Shapiro said he saw. "Did you happen to notice whether he left his drink on a table when he moved around the room?"

"So somebody could put poison in it? Is that what this is all about? Seeing he's dead? Yes, I guess he did—I couldn't swear to it, though."

He wasn't being asked to swear to anything. Merely to give his best recollection. He had given it. So. Did he happen to remember about what time Branson started emptying ashtrays? If,

136

as he gathered, Branson had indeed done that, bringing the party to an end.

Sam did remember that Branson had begun to empty ashtrays. He and this butler guy. Sam had thought it rather odd. It had been only a little after midnight.

"We'd have done it," Sam Scanlon said, "Otto and I. Like always. Part of the job. Leave everything cleaned up. Ashtrays empty, glasses washed. Well, rinsed out, anyway. Right, Mr. Owen?"

"Essential part of the service," Owen said. "Leave everything shipshape."

"Apparently Mr. Branson didn't want to wait," Shapiro said. "Maybe he—oh, just got sleepy. Wanted to call it a night. A little after midnight, as you remember it, Mr. Scanlon?"

Sam thought so. Perhaps fifteen or twenty minutes past.

"And Lord was helping him?"

Sam said, "The Lord?"

"Not 'the.' Edgar Lord—the dresser. The one you think of as the butler."

"Oh, him. Yes, he was lending a hand. Had been doing that all evening. Seeing that Mr. Branson got everything he wanted, mostly. But helping me keep an eye on glasses, too."

Tony supposed that, except for Branson, the others had ice in their drinks? Sure, except the ones who were drinking champagne. So, Branson's glass would be easy to identify, if Branson left it on a table while he circulated? Sam supposed so. "Was that the way somebody did it?" Sam asked again. "Put poison in his drink?"

"It could have been," Shapiro told him. And added he supposed Sam hadn't seen anyone doing that? Opening a twist of paper, say, and spilling something out of it into Mr. Branson's glass? Sam sure as hell had not. About what time would it have been?

"A little before midnight, probably."

No. They had been busy then. "People were getting thirsty, you know. Looked like the party was really getting going. Figured it would be good for a couple more hours, anyway. O.K. with Otto and me. We get paid by the hour. Right, Mr. Owen?"

Owen agreed that Sam and Otto got paid by the hour, as did the Greenwich Catering Service.

And Lord was still around at midnight, or a little before?

"He sure was. Passing around drinks. Until his boss started on the ashtrays. Like I said, then he started to help the boss."

Had Branson seemed all right when he started to clean things up? Not, say, half asleep?

Sam hadn't noticed anything one way or the other about Branson—only what he was doing. Sam himself had started carrying used glasses out to the kitchen and rinsing them off.

14

They got a cab on Sixth Avenue and rode to the offices of Homicide, Manhattan South. The desk sergeant on the ground floor had envelopes for each of them. Delivered by messenger. Each envelope contained two tickets to that evening's performance of *Summer Solstice* at the Rolf Simon Theater. The tickets, all in the orchestra, were marked $20. Tony could remember when orchestra seats cost four-forty, except for big musicals—those cost five-fifty. Nathan could remember when a seat for a nonmusical went for three dollars and thirty cents—as mentioned by Rolf Simon.

They climbed stairs to Homicide South and checked in. It lacked only half an hour of four o'clock, which was the time for them to check out. Technically, of course. Tony started for his squad-room desk, but Nathan said, "Come along," and they went into his small office. There was a desk, with desk chair, in the office, and an unwelcoming visitor's chair. They sat down and lighted cigarettes, and Nathan said, "So?"

"Lord lied to us," Tony said. "Why?"

"To wipe himself out of the whole business," Shapiro said. "He wasn't even around when it happened. He didn't put sleeping medicine in his employer's glass and has no way of knowing who did. Because he had gone to bed."

"Yes," Tony said. "He had retired, as he probably would put

139

it. How quickly would the barbiturate have acted, do you think?"

Shapiro shrugged wide, thin shoulders. Half an hour or so, he supposed. But that would be for someone with a normal reaction, and would depend on the barbiturate used; some worked faster than others. Would depend too on the amount ingested. Only Branson didn't have the normal reaction. Sleeping pills hit him harder, and it might be they would also hit him quicker. Perhaps Dr. Nelson could help—when he finished with his cadaver.

"Yeah," Tony said. "But not so quick that he didn't start redding up." He paused. "Word my mother used to use," he added.

"I've heard it," Shapiro said. He frowned. "Some kind of blind instinct? Drugged? Clean up, get to bed. Makes you wonder." His shrug was almost a shiver. Oh, well, they could always ask Dr. Nelson.

A telephone call to the Medical Examiner's office proved that wrong. Dr. Nelson was working on a cadaver and was not to be disturbed. "Would anyone else do, Lieutenant?"

Shapiro thought not. It would be guesswork, anyway, and the exact times were not, at the moment, so crucially important.

"Who gains?" he said. "Who stands to profit? And, of course, who loses from Branson's death?"

Tony was quick to answer. "This Price guy; he gets the leading role that Branson had. Prestige, and a jump in salary. And Mrs. Barnes, for fifty thousand. And a couple of other ex-wives, only they weren't at the party. And Lord, who was."

"For longer than he said, apparently. At the party, not in his room, when somebody put a barbiturate in Branson's drink."

"Yes," Shapiro said. "At the time we guess somebody did. I wonder why he lied, don't you, Tony? Being upstairs, of course

140

he couldn't have done anything. Or seen somebody do something."

"Yeah. In high school I had a math teacher who used to put equations on the blackboard and then say to the class, 'What conclusion would a wooden Indian draw?' He thought we were all wooden Indians."

Nathan said, "Yes, Tony, I get your point."

"Simon? He gets out of a contract he'd been trying to buy up. Ten thousand a week, for God's sake. Hell, that figures out at more than a thousand a show, counting matinees."

"Yes, Tony. As a wooden Indian would notice, Simon does save money. Quite a lot of it, it would seem. But with a risk to his advance sale, wouldn't you say? Could be, people will be wanting their money back, couldn't it? We'll know better after tonight, if Simon gets the critics back, I suppose. We—"

The telephone rang, the interoffice telephone. Shapiro answered it. He said, "Yes, Cap—Inspector, Tony and I each got a pair. . . . Well, say we're treading water. . . . Why, yes, we'd like that a lot. . . . Six thirty, then. . . . And mine to Mrs. Weigand. Be seeing you, Inspector."

"He got tickets too," Shapiro told Tony Cook. "Anyway, his wife did. As Dorian Hunt. So she can do sketches for the *Chronicle,* Bill says. And they want Rose and me at their place for an early dinner. To celebrate, he says. His making deputy inspector, I guess."

He looked at his watch and found it was well after four. The afternoon had dissolved around them. With what accomplished? Not much. Water treading was all, probably.

The four-to-midnight shift was on. Shapiro and Cook signed out. Nathan went home to Brooklyn, to tell Rose they were going to the Weigands' for dinner and then to the theater. Tony

141

went to Gay Street. Rachel came out of the shower at the sound of his moving around in her apartment. Yes, she'd be happy to go to the theater for the reopening of *Summer Solstice*. Yes, Hugo's would be fine for dinner. And yes, she'd remember to put clothes on. Ready in, say, half an hour? No, they'd better wait until they were dressed for the quick one.

*   *   *   *   *

The Shapiros' seats were on the aisle, fifth row, in the center section of the orchestra of the Rolf Simon Theater. They were in them by seven fifty-five, in anticipation of the eight-o'clock curtain. And the orchestra was barely half full. The Weigands were in the third row, center, not on the aisle, and Dorian had a sketch pad in her lap. At seven fifty-eight, Nathan stood up and Rose shifted sideways in her seat to let Tony and Rachel Farmer in to the third and fourth seats in the row.

"House seats," Tony said to Rose, beside him. "Did us proud, didn't he?"

"Mr. Simon?" Rose said. "Yes, he did. And Nathan is now an acting captain. Altogether, a proud evening." Then Nathan and Tony stood up again, and Rachel and Rose twisted sideways, to let four people, one of them an outstandingly bulky woman, go by to seats near the center of the row. The men sat down and had to get up almost at once to let another couple through. Their seats were beyond those of the previous two couples, and it was a tight squeeze for them to get past the bulky woman.

"That ought to do it from our side," Nathan said to Rose.

It didn't. There were still two more couples to go at eight-oh-five. The curtain was still down. "We could have finished our coffee," Rachel told Tony. "I said they'd be late."

The orchestra was almost full by eight ten. But two aisle seats in the fourth row, in front of the Shapiros and Tony and Rachel, were still empty.

142

Critics' seats, probably," Rachel said to Tony, keeping her voice low. "Mr. Simon will be—" she left it there.

An usher came down the aisle followed by a tall man in a dark suit. He was alone. He accepted the ticket stub from the usher and sat in the seat on the aisle.

"The man from the *Chronicle*," Rachel said. "He said, 'The rest of the cast was barely adequate,' about the little number I was in a couple of weeks ago. The one you didn't see, Tony, because it closed so fast. I was pretty much the rest of the cast. I and—"

The house lights went down. Slowly, the curtain went up.

The set was, as the program had promised, *The terrace room of the Derwent house in East Hampton, Long Island.* Kenneth Price was alone on the stage. He wore a white dinner jacket. He lighted a cigarette and almost at once, and impatiently, crushed it out in a tray. He crossed the stage to a bar and lifted the lid of an ice bucket on it and, apparently satisfied that there was ice available, slapped the lid back on. Then he said, "Damn!" and crossed toward a door, stage left. But when he had taken only a few steps, that door opened and Arlene Collins came through it into the terrace room of the Derwent house in East Hampton, Long Island. She wore a white, off-the-shoulders dinner dress and she was lovely—poised and lovely. She said, "Happy birthday, darling."

Price said, "At last. I was about to give you up."

She said, "Were you really, darling?"

He crossed to her and put his hands gently on her shoulders. He looked down at her for several seconds. Then he said, "No, child, I guess not. I guess I never will. I'm afraid you're stuck—"

She did not let him finish. She shook her head with resolution. She put both of her hands on his, and they stood so for a mo-

143

ment. Then she said, "It's only seven fifteen, and we said seven-ish. And we do know the Fosters, don't we? Fifteen minutes, at the least. More likely—" She shrugged slightly, her hands still on his.

"Yes," Kenneth Price said to Arlene Collins, except that he was no longer Kenneth Price, nor she Arlene Collins, "time for one of our own."

He released her and went to the bar. "A very little one," she said. "A soupçon, whatever that may be." He poured, very little liquid into one glass and more into another. He carried both glasses to a sofa, stage right, and they sat close together and clicked glasses.

"Happy birthday, dear," Mrs. Louis Derwent said to her husband.

They were doing it well, Nathan thought. Not that he was any judge, of course. He looked at Rose, and she gave him a quick nod.

A young man in a black dinner jacket appeared on the terrace beyond the room. He was separated from the room by sliding glass doors. "Ronald, and by himself," Derwent said, and went to the doors and slid one of them open. The young man, Ronald Foster by the program, came into the room. He said, "Hi. I bring apologies from sainted parents. Dad got held up at the office. Just got home. And will you two meet them in about half an hour at the Carousel, instead of their coming here first? And happy solstice to you both."

The actor playing Ronald Foster—Peter somebody, wasn't he?—seemed younger than Nathan remembered him from rehearsals. Now he was about Arlene Collins's age, which was evidently the early twenties. And Kenneth Price, as Derwent, looked slightly older than Nathan had thought him. Of course. Grayed hair at the temples.

144

Derwent returned to his seat on the sofa but not, this time, as close to his wife as he had sat before. Ronald Foster sat in a chair in front of them, a glass-topped table separating them. Seated so, they formed a triangle. Which, Nathan realized, had been the director's intention.

"Happy solstice and happy birthday," Ronald said. "I am right, aren't I?" He paused an instant, and added "sir" to his sentence. A most polite and formal young man, paying light deference to a senior. And with a tinge of Harvard in his speech. Or, perhaps, stage Oxford. Ronald was not, Nathan assumed, a character of whom the audience was supposed to grow greatly fond. Price, after playing Ronald when Clive Branson had the lead, must find the switch in roles rather gratifying.

"Quite right, Ron," Louis Derwent said to Ronald Foster. "Summer and I began together. When the sun had passed its zenith. Beware the twenty-first of June."

"Not beware, darling. Celebrate." That was from Mrs. Derwent—Carol, from the program. She lifted her glass in a salute. The Derwents clicked glasses. Ronald Foster held his out across the table, and Carol Derwent held hers out toward his. The glasses did not really touch.

The three talked, then, about a racehorse, which it appeared the Derwents owned, and about politics, but at first only briefly. The conversation was light, agile, now and then witty. The wit was most often Louis Derwent's, although Carol had some shimmering lines. Laughter began to ripple through the audience.

Information about the Derwents seeped out of the dialogue. The summer solstice, which that day was, was also Louis Derwent's birthday. "Forth-two years ago today," Derwent said. "In the late afternoon, they tell me. The baby who came for cocktails."

"Twenty years before me," Carol said to that. "But you waited for me, didn't you, dear?"

"Twenty years and six months," Derwent said. "December twenty-first to the summer solstice. We try to make things come out even, Ron. Not that they always do, of course."

He turned as the door through which Carol had come on stage opened again. This time Helen Barnes came into the set. She, too, wore a dinner dress. Hers was of pale yellow, long-sleeved and close-fitting. The result was admirable. The two men stood up when she came into the room. She said, "I thought your father and mother, Ron—"

"So did I, Mrs. Ashley," young Foster said. "So did they. Only, as usual, Dad got held up, so we're meeting at the restaurant."

"Parents!" Mrs. Ashley said. "So unreliable. So trying, really."

To that, Carol Derwent said, "*Mother!*"

Her husband added, "Come off it, Mary. The usual?"

She said, "Please, son," and Derwent went to the bar and emptied crushed ice from a glass which had waited with the ice chilling it. He poured a pale liquid into the glass.

"Perhaps we ought to go," Carol said. "You did say about half an hour, Ronald."

"Parents can wait," Ronald Foster assured her. "Be good for them, actually."

They sat down again, Mary Ashley on the sofa next to her son-in-law, Ronald Foster where he had sat before. The four sipped from their glasses and again talked. And again, to Nathan's ears, the dialogue shimmered. And the laughter from the audience grew more frequent. Some of it was drawn by Ronald's needling Louis about his racehorse, and by Louis's wittily insulting answers. The skillful building of the horse into a plot is-

146

sue was interrupted at a high point of suspense by Carol. As she spoke and stood up, the others stood too. With Louis delivering one last shot at Ronald, the four of them went out to the terrace and turned away out of sight. The curtain came down and the house lights went up, slowly. End of Act One.

The audience stirred. Sections of it moved up aisles toward cigarettes in the lobby. Act one had been, Nathan thought, quick and light and pleasant. He decided he needed a cigarette. Rose decided she didn't. Tony and Rachel were talking with animation. Nathan Shapiro went up the aisle alone.

At first the man standing behind the central section of seats seemed only vaguely familiar. He was tall and thin and wore a dark-blue suit. He wore a white shirt with, surprisingly, a stiff white collar. He wore a black string tie.

"Evening, Mr. Lord," Nathan said. "Enjoying the show?"

"Just dropped in for a glimpse, Lieutenant," Edgar Lord, dresser to the late Clive Branson, assured Shapiro. "They do know me here, of course. Passed me in for a few minutes, Brian did. He's one of the doormen."

Nathan said he saw.

"Mr. Price seems to be doing quite well in the part," Lord said. "Not the authority Mr. Branson had, of course. But quite adequate, it seems to me. You agree, sir?"

"Seems all right to me," Nathan said. "Not that I'm any judge. Not at all my line of country."

Lord said, "No, sir," with what Nathan took to be commiseration in his tone. "Well, I'd better get back to the dressing room. Pick up this package Mr. Price called me about. He's got a change for the second, but he's probably made it by now. Got our number somehow."

"Package?" Shapiro said.

"Mr. Branson's stage makeup, Lieutenant. Left it in Dressing

147

Room One, of course. And Mr. Price is there now." Lord looked sad. "Mr. Price thought I might as well pick it up. Though I don't know what to do with it when I do. I don't suppose the police would want it, would they, sir?"

"I don't think so," Shapiro told him. "Just take it on back to the house. You're still staying there, Lord?"

Lord had thought he was supposed to, at least until the police had finished their investigation of Mr. Branson's sad death.

The police did expect Lord to stay on in the Murray Hill house, Shapiro told the neatly dressed, spruced-up Edgar Lord. And to keep the police informed of his whereabouts if he left it—as a matter of form only, of course, in case there turned out to be more quesitons they wanted to ask him. About the Sunday night party, perhaps, at which he had been present for so short a time.

"I want to explain about that, Lieutenant. I'm afraid I gave you a wrong impression. Mr. Branson did tell me I could retire. That was around eleven, I can't say to the minute. And I did go up to my room, sir. But—well, I came back down again. To—to help out. There were only two men from the catering place and—well, I felt it was part of my duty to be around to help. Part of my service to Mr. Branson, if you know what I mean. So I came down again. A little before midnight, I should think. And—helped them. Passed drinks. That sort of thing. I'm sorry I didn't remember to tell you earlier, sir."

And hadn't, Shapiro thought, remembered earlier that the caterer's men would be likely to mention his helping hands. So—nothing of importance, unless, around midnight, Lord had seen or heard anything which might be of interest to the police. Had he?

"Oh, no, sir," Lord said.

The lights in the lobby dimmed, went up again, and dimmed again and again went up.

"Second-act warning," Lord said, as people began to drift

toward their seats. "I may as well go get Mr. Branson's make-up."

"The package Mr. Price telephoned you about. This afternoon, that would have been?"

"About five, sir. I'd just made myself a cup of tea, you know."

"Yes," Shapiro said. "Say where he was calling from?"

Price had not. And, no, there had been no background sound. Not that he was aware of, anyway. Did it matter?

"I can't see how it would," Shapiro told him, and joined the parade down the aisle. He never had got the cigarette he had come out for. On the other hand, he had got a statement from Lord which cleared up a discrepancy, or appeared to.

Edgar Lord went out through the lobby, presumably on his way to the stage door and a package in Dressing Room 1.

The curtain went up. Same set. Only Mrs. Ashley and Carol Ashley Derwent were onstage. Mary Ashley was at the bar, but seemed to be merely leaning against it. Both women were dressed for tennis, Carol in shorts which revealed tanned and graceful legs. Mary wore a short white dress which did not conceal legs of equal grace, if somewhat less tan. For some seconds, neither woman said anything. Nathan looked down at his program. *The Derwents' terrace room. The next afternoon.*

"Well, child, it's your life," Mrs. Ashley said to her daughter. "I hope you've learned to take care of it, learned that Louis Derwents don't grow on every tree. It must be hot as hell on the court. I hope the two of them—well, one of them, anyway, doesn't get—"

She did not finish. Derwent and Foster appeared on the terrace. Both men carried tennis rackets and were dressed accordingly. Young Foster mopped his face with a small towel. Derwent slid a glass door open, and the two came into the terrace room. Foster said, "Whew!"

"Spoken for both of us," Derwent said. "Summer has come

149

most promptly upon its hour. Your turn, ladies."

"Mixed doubles?" the older—but just perceptibly older—woman asked.

"If you hold out for them," Louis Derwent told his mother-in-law. "I was rather thinking of a cold shower. However—"

"*I* don't hold out," Mrs. Ashley told him. "A long cold drink will do as well. But . . . the children?"

"Having just been given a tennis lesson," young Foster said. "I can skip—unless you want to rally a bit, Carol?"

"For about five minutes," Carol Derwent said. "If it's as hot as you two look."

She went to one of the chairs and picked up a tennis racket lying on it. Foster held the door open for her and followed her out to the terrace. They went right, out of view.

"Youth will be served heat prostration," Price, speaking as Louis Derwent, said. There was something intended in his tone, Shapiro thought. Envy? Perhaps wistfulness?

"And welcome to it, Louis," Mary Ashley said. "Come off it, dear. Fix us both gin and tonics, why don't you?"

Derwent was putting ice into tall glasses and reaching for a bottle when there was a tap on Shapiro's shoulder. The tapper was a uniformed patrolman. He bent down to say something, but Nathan Shapiro stood and went up the aisle, the patrolman following him. In the lobby, Shapiro stopped and said, "Yes?" to the patrolman.

"Probably just a mugging," the patrolman said. "But seeing he worked for this Branson guy, the sergeant thought we'd better—"

"Yes," Shapiro said. "He was quite right. "How bad is it, officer?"

"Head wound, Lieutenant. Taking him to Bellevue. He was wearing a derby hat, for God's sake."

150

The victim had been identified by the stage doorman as Edgar Lord, dresser to Clive Branson. The attack had been made just outside the stage door, which was in an alleyway between the theater and the building next it. The alleyway was well lighted; it was not much frequented when a performance was going on. If provided seclusion of sorts for a mugger but, Shapiro thought, a scarcity of prey.

Tony Cook came out into the lobby. Nathan told him what had happened, and about the derby hat. Tony said, "Jesus *Christ!*" and added, "My father used to wear them. When I was just a small boy. They were going out of style even then. Before all hats pretty much did."

"I know," Shapiro said. "See what you can get from Bellevue, Tony. I'll see what we can pick up here. Though chances are it was just a mugging. Only—" He let it hang there and went out of the lobby and down the alleyway to the stage door. There were a couple more uniformed men there, one of them a sergeant. The sergeant was talking to a civilian in his sixties. Nathan showed the police sergeant his shield. The sergeant said, "Figured you'd want in on it, Lieutenant. This is Brian O'Leary, sir. Identified the victim for us."

"Ed Lord it was, Lieutenant. Was Mr. Branson's dresser, you know."

"Yes," Shapiro said. "You let him in this evening. I take it."

"Saw him go in's more like it," O'Leary said. "Came in and out a lot, way dressers do. Went into Dressing Room One, the room Mr. Branson used to use. Too bad about Branson. He was a pretty famous guy. In the profession, I mean."

Shapiro agreed it was too bad about Clive Branson. He said, "You saw Lord go into this dressing room. Did you see him come out again? And was he carrying anything?"

O'Leary had not seen Lord come out of the dressing room.

151

The next he had seen of Lord, he was lying on the pavement just outside the stage door.

"That hat he wore was all smashed in," O'Leary said. "And he was bleeding pretty bad around the head. I said something— 'You all right, Mr. Lord?' or something, though I could see he sure as hell wasn't all right. He didn't say anything, so I went back in and called the cops. The police I mean, Lieutenant. They came real quick and then the ambulance came. Didn't use the siren much, I'll say that for the ambulance guys. Not enough to be heard inside, I guess. By the audience, I mean."

"This was after the second act had started?" Shapiro asked the doorman.

It had been. Maybe five minutes after the curtain had gone up.

"There wasn't a package beside Mr. Lord? As if he had been carrying it when he was attacked?"

There hadn't been.

"What's this about a package?" the sergeant asked.

"Lord had come to pick up a package from Branson's—or what was Branson's—dressing room," Shapiro said. "What Lord told me, anyway."

"No package when we got here, Lieutenant. The mugger probably took it. He emptied the guy's pockets. Would there have been anything valuable in this package?"

"Only Branson's stage makeup, way I got it," Shapiro said. No kind of haul for a mugger, which probably the attacker was. Probably just a mugger. Then, presumably, just a coincidence. Nathan Shapiro does not like coincidences. They get in the way.

Shapiro said, "Get anything, Tony?" without needing to look at Tony Cook.

152

15

Tony had got what Bellevue had, which was nothing conclusive.
Edgar Lord was still alive. He was in surgery, his condition
critical. He had a fractured skull. If he survived, it probably
would be thanks to the derby hat he was wearing. The antique
hat, the "bowler." Part of the proper costume of a dresser? A
gentleman's valet?

Lord had been hit from behind, apparently with a narrow
metal rod or something of the kind. The rod had crushed the
derby hat and laid Lord's head open. It had also cracked his
skull. They might be able to put a plate in. Time, and surgical
skill, and luck, would show. At best, it would be several weeks
before Lord could tell them anything. If he remembered anything, which most probably he would not.

"Price telephoned him this afternoon," Shapiro said. "About
five o'clock, Lord told me. Asked him to come and pick up Branson's makeup from the dressing room. The room Price is using
now."

Shapiro stopped speaking. His forehead wrinkled slightly.
Tony, who is familiar with the Shapiro expressions, waited.

"Just remembered something," Nathan said. "Didn't think
anything about it when Lord said it. He said Price had got hold
of the number 'somehow.'"

"The telephone number, I suppose." Tony said. "An unlisted

153

number, you think he meant? One Price wouldn't be able to look up? And hadn't been given?"

"Could be, couldn't it?" Shapiro said. "Just could be, Tony. With Price maybe not one of the privileged ones, far as Lord knew. We'd better check it out, hadn't we?"

There was a telephone booth backstage, O'Leary told them. Near the stage door, sure. He'd show them.

He did. It was complete with Manhattan directory.

There were quite a few Bransons with Manhattan telephone numbers. But none of them was named Clive and none lived in the Murray Hill area.

Tony used the phone to find out that, yes, the number for Clive Branson, at the address he gave in Murray Hill, was unlisted.

"We'll ask Price about it after the show," Shapiro said. "And whether it was actually he who called Lord."

"You think it wasn't?"

Shapiro didn't know. Lord apparently had had no doubts. The caller evidently had identified himself as Kenneth Price. Perhaps Lord had recognized his voice. But they couldn't ask Edgar Lord about that. Not now and perhaps not ever. So—who would know Branson's unlisted number?

Rolf Simon, probably. Martha Abel, almost certainly, since Branson had been her client. Bret Askew? They'd have to ask him.

"He's in the theater," Tony said. "Standing behind the orchestra section. Saw him as I came out."

"Wants to see how it's going," Shapiro said. "Means a lot to him, of course. And a lot to Mr. Simon. See him around now, Tony?"

Tony did not, which meant nothing. Almost certainly he had been around, if only to see whether the reviewers had decided to cover this reopening. As the man from the *Chronicle* had. "Came back for the second act, too," Tony said. "And Mrs. Abel's here," Tony added. "To see how her boy's making out."

On the chance it hadn't been Price who had telephoned Lord, making sure that Lord would be in the stage-door alleyway at a time convenient for a "mugger," they had better ask around about Branson's unlisted telephone number. Find out how widely it had been circulated.

"Seen Mr. Simon around this evening?" Shapiro asked O'Leary, who was just inside the stage door, taking everything in.

O'Leary sure as hell had. Mr. Simon had been backstage during the first act. "Likes to keep an eye on things, Mr. Simon does. Him and Kirby—the director, you know. Far's I know, Mr. Simon's still around somewhere. Could be—oh."

"What's going on here?" Rolf Simon wanted to know as he came into the corridor which led from backstage to the stage door. "Oh, it's you, Lieutenant. Still hanging around?"

"Still," Shapiro agreed, and told Simon what was going on, what had gone on.

To which Simon said, "Jeez—there's a jinx on this thing. But the *Chronicle* guy did show. *And* came back for Act Two, believe it or not." Simon stepped out into the alleyway and lighted a cigarette. "Not that it isn't too bad about old Lord," he said. "Been around a long time, the old boy had. What was he doing here tonight?"

Shapiro told him what Lord had been doing, or had said he'd been doing. And about the telephone call which had brought him there.

Simon said, "Mmm." He added, "Didn't know Price had the Branson telephone number. Didn't spread it around much, the old boy didn't. Didn't want fans bothering him, way he put it.

155

And he did have fans, Lieutenant. Maybe not as many as he thought he had, but he had them. Reason Askew was so set on our getting him for the show. Not that I didn't agree. I'm not saying I didn't. Or that his name didn't help the advance."

Asked, he said sure he had Branson's unlisted number. He supposed Mrs. Abel had it, since she was his agent. Askew?

"Maybe. I don't know. Wait a minute. When I was trying to buy up Branson's contract at a decent figure, Askew offered to help persuade the old boy. Said he'd give him a ring and got his number from me. Thing is, those damned reviews scared our playwright. Scared me too, come to that. And I ought to have had more sense. Spotted it in the rehearsals, instead of keeping on thinking maybe he'd shape up when there was an audience out front. After all, the old boy was a pro. Thing is, after a point you're stuck with it. See what I mean?"

A little vaguely, Shapiro did see.

"It was different when we had out-of-town tryouts," Simon said. "You could cut your losses and not bring it in. Now, like I said, you get stuck with it. Lot of money tied up in it. Get what I mean?"

Shapiro said he did, he guessed. "Mr. Askew agreed with you in the end?" he asked. "That Branson was miscast for the part?"

"He sure did. Did a complete turnabout. Hell, he even offered to put up part of the money to buy up Branson's contract. If we could persuade the old boy that run-of-the-play didn't mean forever."

"Askew was ready to chip in? I take it he had the money?"

"Rolling in it, Lieutenant. The Askew Foundation, that's his family."

"Then the success of *Summer Solstice* didn't mean all that much to him, I suppose?"

Simon looked at him with apparent astonishment, mixed with

pity. "Man," he said, "you don't know them, do you? Writers, particularly those who write plays—hell, man, they're nuts. Even the best of them. There's a saying that only a fool writes, except for money. Partly, it's true, I suppose, but only partly. Thing is, they're an egotistical bunch. Want to be well thought of. Want to be famous. 'Not *the* Mr. Jones!' Or Mr. Askew. Oh, we've got to have them in my business, I'll give you that. Just like we have to have actors. But, by and large, they're all bats— writers *and* actors. Been driving me nuts for years."

Neither Cook nor Shapiro said anything to that.

Simon closed his eyes for a moment. Then he said, "All right, maybe I'm not fair to them. Maybe it's not just the acclaim they're looking for. Maybe it's something inside them. Pride, maybe. Just doing a job and knowing you've done it well. It could be that way with Bret Askew. Not that he'll turn down the money, you understand. Takes his royalty cut, all right. And, with luck, it'll be plenty—if it catches on, like maybe it will with Price playing the lead. And if the *Chronicle* guy comes through. And he did come back for the second act, didn't he?"

"Tell me more about Askew, Mr. Simon."

"What's more to tell? Nice enough kid. And he can write. Two or three off-Broadway things got good enough notices. This is his first big one. Means a lot to him. Does to me too, of course. But—well, I've had my share of hits. Been at it long enough, God knows. Askew, he hasn't. Needs one to—to lift him up. And I'll say this for the kid, he could have put it on himself, put up the money; wouldn't have noticed it with what he's probably got. I asked him once why he'd brought the script to me instead of producing it himself. And, mmm, he said a lot of nice things about me, how he'd always admired what I'd done, that sort of thing. Then he said, 'Ever hear of vanity press, Mr. Simon?' I said yes, I had, but that was used by people who write novels,

157

who pay to have their books published. A racket, mostly, I'd think. But then I pretty much knew what he was going to say next. And he said it—said that putting on your own play was pretty much the same thing and would be something only amateurs would do. And he was right, wasn't he? For that matter, it has happened in the theater—not often, and years ago—but plays, one or two anyway, have been subsidized by their authors. By amateurs, like he said."

Simon looked at his watch.

"Maybe five minutes to go," he said. "I better be getting back inside. Have a look at the audience. Count the calls."

He went back into the theater. They watched him go. After a bit, they went in after him. From backstage they could hear the applause. It was loud and sustained. There were even a few cheers, somewhat subdued. They found they were in one of the wings and stopped just in time. "Damn near took curtain calls ourselves, didn't we?" Tony said, his voice low.

A couple of inadvertent steps more and they would have, intruding on Arlene Collins and Kenneth Price, who were downstage center, holding hands and bowing to the audience. Price released the girl's hand and she moved back a step. He bowed to her. She returned the bow with a curtsy. The curtain came down.

The two left by way of the terrace. The applause continued. Helen Barnes and the young actor who played Foster went to the front of the stage and took bows. The applause spurted up, but only briefly. The curtain went down again, and then the applause increased. There was a short interval, and then Ken Price and Arlene Collins came on from the terrace hand in hand (and trying, Nathan thought, to look reluctant) to take another call.

People in the audience were standing up by then and moving toward the aisles. The curtain came down. The applause trickled away. Shapiro and Cook went on backstage and waited outside the door of Dressing Room 1.

They did not have long to wait. Price—wearing the white dinner jacket again—came offstage and was opening the dressing-room door when he saw the two tall detectives. He said, "Evening," but the tone was *You again?* Then he said, "Want to see me?"

"A couple of questions," Shapiro said. "About Edgar Lord."

Price said, "Lord?" with a question in his voice. Then he said, "Oh, Clive Branson's dresser, isn't he? What about him?"

Shapiro told him what about Edgar Lord. Price said, *"Jesus Christ,"* and then, "Why me, Lieutenant? Think I mugged him?"

"Just a couple of questions?" Shapiro said.

They were told to come on in and "watch me get this muck off my face."

They followed him into the room. It was larger than Helen Barnes's to which Nathan had climbed one flight up. Price sat at the dressing table and began to tissue makeup from his face. He said, "I didn't hit Lord over the head with a blunt instrument. Or a sharp one, if that's what it was. I was onstage. Acting, you know. Or maybe, changing—without a dresser of my own, incidentally. Not that I won't be hiring one. Anyway—how do I fit in?"

"You did telephone Lord this afternoon? Ask him to come to the theater—to this dressing room—to pick up Branson's makeup?"

Price wheeled abruptly from the dressing table to face the detectives. "What the hell gave you that crazy idea, Lieutenant?"

"Lord gave it to me, Mr. Price—an hour or so ago, here in the theater. Told me that was what had happened. You say it didn't?"

"I sure as hell do. I didn't telephone him. You want to know where Branson's makeup is?" He had stood up while speaking and crossed to where some clothes were hanging and took a shoe box from a shelf above the clothes. He took the lid off the box and held the box out to Shapiro.

Shapiro had no reason to doubt that the miscellany he saw in the box was Branson's makeup. He said, "I see. It was in your way, evidently. But you didn't—"

Price's interruption was vehement. "I had other things on my mind. Tonight's performance—"

"Then," Shapiro said, "someone must have lied to Lord. Identified himself as you and asked him to pick up the makeup."

"Or Lord may have lied to you." Price set the box down at one end of the dressing table and sat in front of the table again. "To explain his being here."

"Possibly, of course. Although I don't see why he should, do you? No need I can see for his explaining why he came to the theater. Wanting to see how you did in Branson's old role would be reason enough. Don't you agree?"

Price turned back to the mirror and resumed dabbing at his face. After a few seconds, he said, "All right. Somebody called Lord, pretending to be me, and got him up here so he could kill him. Is that what you think?"

"Assuming you didn't make the call yourself, yes."

"You can damn well assume I didn't."

"All right. Did you know Branson had an unlisted telephone number? And did you know what it was?"

"No to both questions. But I'm not surprised the old boy had an unlisted number. Didn't want his hordes of fans calling him at all hours." Abruptly he turned back from the makeup mirror and again faced Shapiro. "Listen," he said, "I didn't mean that the way it sounded. The hordes-of-fans bit. As if I were quoting

160

something he'd said, or maybe thought. He was a nice old guy. No more ego than—well, than the rest of us. Actors aren't precisely noted for modesty. And damn it all, Branson had no reason to be modest. He was one hell of an actor. In his day, anyway."

"Which, I take it, you agree had passed?"

"To play Louis Derwent, yes. Derwent is in his early forties. Askew makes a point of it. Actually, he pretty much made his play of it. Branson was somewhere in his sixties. Makeup can do a lot, sure . . . but there are limits. Simon or Bob Kirby, or somebody, should have spotted that during rehearsals. Hell, it stuck out to me. And I haven't their experience."

"And," Tony Cook said, "you thought you could play the part better than he was doing?"

Price laughed, rather harshly. He did not answer directly. "I didn't kill poor old Lord," he said. "Also, I didn't kill Branson to get his role in *Summer Solstice*. And yes, it's a good part and I like playing it. And playing it will give me a step up in the profession, to say nothing of more money from Rolf Simon. About half as much as the ten he was paying Branson, but a lot more than he was paying me to understudy and play young Foster. All right. I still didn't kill Branson—or his dresser."

"All right, Mr. Price. That tennis racket you carry on stage. Does it happen to have a steel frame?"

Price said, "Huh?" Then he said, "Hell. It's just a prop. Can't say I ever noticed. It's right over there, by the door. Look at it yourself. You mean, it wasn't a blunt object Lord was hit with? Killed with?"

"Lord isn't dead, Mr. Price. Yet, anyway. He was wearing a derby hat which apparently cushioned the blow."

Shapiro went to the doorway and picked up the tennis racket. It did have a steel frame. And one of the strings was broken. He

161

raised the racket to the serving position. It was fairly heavy. He brought it down in what would have been a hard serve; only he turned its face so that the steel frame whipped down like a thin steel rod. It hit nothing, of course, as he checked what would have been a blow.

"Could have been that way, I guess," Price said. "Only like I said, not by me."

"We'll have to take the racket along," Shapiro said. "Have it examined. See what broke the string. Strain on the frame, could be. Have to get another one for tomorrow night, I'm afraid."

"No problem, Lieutenant. Assuming I'm not in jail." His inflection was light. It was a joke, or almost a joke.

"If you're not in jail," Shapiro agreed. There was no inflection in his voice. "One other thing, Mr. Price. Mind telling us where you were yesterday afternoon? From four o'clock on, say. As a matter of routine. The sort of question they want us to ask."

"They" are the unidentified rulers in Shapiro's terminology. "They" are demanding superiors. They are never named.

"In Mrs. Abel's apartment. And yes, she has a telephone. And no, I didn't use it."

"All right."

"And probably she knows Branson's unlisted number. And could have given it to me."

"Yes, Mr. Price. We'll ask her about that."

"So?"

"That's all for now, Mr. Price. For the moment, let's say. We'll have to ask Mrs. Abel. Try to find out who else knew this unlisted telephone number."

They left the dressing room, Tony carrying the steel tennis racket. Outside, they arranged for its delivery to the police lab. "Might as well give Bellevue another buzz," Shapiro said. "And

162

tell Mrs. Abel we'll come around to see her. In half an hour or so."

Tony Cook went to the nearby telephone booth. He came out of it. "Critical," he said. "Touch and go. Sounds more like go, I guess. And Mrs. Abel says O.K."

Tony had Martha Abel's address in the East Seventies. They went to the street to look for a taxicab. It was a long look. Finally a cab came with its top light on. It even stopped for them. "Could be Price is our boy," Tony said as the cab pulled away from the curb.

Shapiro didn't disagree. He didn't agree, either. He said, "Mmm."

"Why not?" Tony said. "Gained a lot. A starring part, or close to it. A lot more money, he says. Not as much as Branson was getting, but a lot more than Price was getting as the Foster twerp. And he had this racked handy—if that was what was used on Lord. And probably he tried to poison Askew with those alkaloids, the ones that dilate the pupils. He's the only one who had a chance."

"Not the only one, Tony. And why?"

"Askew saw something at this party. Saw Price do something. Get him out of the way."

"Only," Shapiro said, "he didn't, did he? Get him out of the way. Just made him a little groggy for a few hours."

"All right, Nate. So he didn't know the dosage."

"Or didn't want Askew dead. The way it looks, maybe nobody did."

"He's still our best bet," Tony Cook said.

Sometimes, challenged, Nathan Shapiro comes through. It is worth trying. This time, it didn't seem to work. They went several blocks and were stopped in traffic before Shapiro answered. Then he said, "Could be Simon, as a way of buying up a con-

163

tract. Could be Mrs. Abel . . . to give Price a boost—she's fond of him, I think. Could even be young Withers."

"Withers?"

"Peter Withers. The boy who's playing Ronald Foster."

Cook said, "Oh." Then he said, "Why?"

"Haven't the foggiest," Shapiro said. "And here we are, apparently."

Where they were was in front of a towering and new-looking apartment house on Seventy-second near Second Avenue. Like the building's exterior, the lobby was new and shining. It contained a counter with a man in uniform behind it. He was gracious with them, although Shapiro suspected he would rather have seen them differently dressed. Black tie, anyway. And who should he say was calling?

Shapiro told him. He omitted the title. The man in uniform used a telephone. It was quickly answered.

"Mrs. Abel is expecting you, Lieutenant." There was a slight note of inquiry on the word *Lieutenant*. "Penthouse A. Third elevator, please."

They went into the third elevator and up, without a stop, to a floor marked 22. From the stopping place, corridors stretched in two directions. One was marked A, and they went along it for thirty feet or so. They came to a door, which was also marked A, and Tony pressed the bell push. Chimes sounded beyond the door, and very quickly a pretty black girl in a dark-green uniform opened the door. She said, "Lieutenant Shapiro?" with a faint note of puzzlement in her voice.

Shapiro admitted that, strange as it might seem, he was Lieutenant Shapiro. "And Detective Cook," he added.

She said, "Gentlemen," and would they please come in.

The room they went into was large and pretty much walled with glass. The lights of Manhattan seemed to be all around

164

them. Beyond the windows on one side of the big room there was a terrace with summer furniture on it. Martha Abel rose from a sofa near a large fireplace set with summer logs. She said, "Lieutenant. And Mr. Cook, isn't it? You make late calls, don't you? It must be almost midnight."

"Yes," Shapiro said. "Sorry to bother you so late. We shouldn't need more than a few minutes."

"It's all right," she said. "I'm a bit of a night owl, actually. Won't you both sit down somewhere?"

She herself sank back onto the sofa. She did so very gracefully and, as gracefully, drew the folds of a deep-green hostess gown around a slim body. Altogether a very graceful lady, Shapiro thought. One living in grace.

"And how can I help you?" she asked. "I suppose it's about poor dear Clive. My late client."

It was, Shapiro told her, but only indirectly. It was about Clive Branson's unlisted telephone number. He assumed she had it?

"Of course, Lieutenant. He was in my stable. I try to keep them—well, tethered. Know where I can reach them in case something comes up, you know."

"Yes," Shapiro said, "I supposed you would. Have you any idea who else might have known this telephone number? Which the Bell people won't give out, of course."

She really didn't know. Not too many, she thought. "Dear Clive was essentially a private person. A few friends, I'd suppose. But I don't actually know who. One or two on the West Coast, probably. People in the studios, I suppose. And my Hollywood office, of course."

"I was thinking of people here," Shapiro told her. "In New York."

"Mr. Simon, I'm sure. Perhaps Mrs. Barnes, who used to be

married to him. One of the several who were, poor dear. I don't know who else he may have given it to."

"Mr. Price?"

"I'd doubt it. They weren't all that chummy, I shouldn't think. But I don't really know."

"Mr. Askew?"

"Yes, I think so. Although I don't know why I do. Something Clive told me about talking to Bret Askew on the phone. Wait, I remember now. It was about the contract. Simon wanted to buy it up, you know, and wanted to do it on the cheap. We weren't having that. Clive was a big name, one of the biggest in the profession. That was why Simon wanted him, wasn't it? And why Askew was so keen on getting him. At least until those nasty, unfair reviews. Then Askew—yes, Clarice?"

The pretty black girl was standing just inside a door into the big room. She carried a silver tray with what, from the distance, looked like a glass of milk on it.

"It's twelve o'clock, Mrs. Abel," the maid said. "It's been two hours."

"Oh, dear," Martha Abel said, "how monotonous. But all right. Put it down here, Clarice. I suppose I have to drink the damn stuff, however I hate it."

The black girl put the tray with the glass, now obviously of milk, on an end table.

Martha said, "Thank you, dear," and then, "Sorry, Lieutenant. My doctor insists. Yes, an ulcer flare-up—the ailment of the profession. Tension, they think it is. Sorry to interrupt. Yes, I think Bret did call Clive. Tried to argue him into being what Mr. Simon called 'reasonable.' Not that it was, of course. Not from our point of view. Fifty thousand. Five weeks for a run of the play. Simon should have known better. He—sorry, it's a dead issue now, of course. Dead issue with a dead man."

166

"Yes," Shapiro said. "Mr. Askew wanted the contract bought up? Tried to talk Branson into selling? And yet you've just said how keen Askew was on getting him in the first place."

"Wanted a big name. A name that would be a draw. Actually, it was Simon who first came to me about Clive, but Askew—yes, Askew was just as keen. As I said. Kept bothering me about it. Getting me to pressure Clive."

"Mr. Branson didn't too much want the role, Mrs. Abel?"

"Oh, he liked the play, but he wasn't sure the part was right for him. Kept pointing out it had been years since he'd played light comedy—years, in fact, since there'd *been* light comedy like *Solstice*. And he kept saying, 'I don't know. I just don't know.' I more or less argued him into it, I'm afraid. And then those nasty notices, making all those remarks about his age."

"They weren't true? I mean you didn't think they were? After all, there was rather a gap between Branson's sixties and Derwent's early forties."

"Nothing his technique didn't take care of. Damn it all, he was an actor. He could play Ken Price off the stage. Not that Ken isn't damn good, too—better than he realizes, in fact. The time I spend trying to build him up! In his own mind, I mean. Take this afternoon. I spent hours talking him out of the jitters about going on tonight. Kept telling him it was in the bag—that he'd be the hit of all time. You saw the play tonight, Lieutenant? And you, Mr. Cook? He *was* good, wasn't he?"

"I thought so," Shapiro said.

"He seemed fine to me," Tony said, "and to the girl I brought with me. And she's in the profession. An actress, I mean."

"He was damn good," Martha Abel said, "and I hope the *Chronicle* man has sense enough to know it. *And* to say it."

She drank from the glass of milk and made a face. She said, "Ugh," but she drank all of it. "There! Now I have two hours' respite. You'd think there'd be something better, wouldn't you? And there is, only my doctor won't give it to me. Says mine is the wrong kind of ulcer. Bret Askew's doctor gives it to him, though. He told me about it. Even gave me the name of it. Only it needs a prescription, and Dr. Alexander won't give me one."

She shook her head. She lighted a cigarette and said, "Sorry— you two didn't come to hear me bellyache about a bellyache. It's that damn milk sets me off."

It was quite all right, Shapiro assured her. As a matter of fact, he'd been having some ulcer trouble himself. If there was some kind of miracle drug for it, he'd like to know what it was, so he could ask his own doctor about it. Did she remember the name of the drug which had worked for Bret Askew?

She had it written down someplace, she thought. She took a little bell from the table and jingled it, and that brought Clarice. "Yes, Mrs. Abel?"

There was a little black book on her desk. Would Clarice bring it to her? And then, after she had let Mr. Price in, Clarice could go to bed. She'd had a long day.

When Clarice brought the little black book, Martha Abel thumbed its pages. "Donnatal Extentabs," she said. She spelled the words out. "One every twelve hours for peptic ulcer," she read. Then she said, "I remember now. Bret told me he'd been having to take a different tablet—or capsule or whatever it was—every four hours. And that every twelve hours was a lot easier to remember."

"Donnatal Extentabs," Shapiro said. "I'll rmember that. Ask my own doctor about it. You said something about your maid's letting Mr. Price in, Mrs. Abel. You mean tonight?"

"Any time now, Lieutenant. For a small celebration. Just the two of us." She smiled. "Yes," she said, "as I'm sure you've guessed, there's more than agent-and-client relationship between

Ken and me. We're friends. Quite good friends, you could say. So we'll celebrate his success tonight. He'll have champagne. And I—well, probably I'll have another glass of milk. Lucky, lucky me."

"This afternoon, Mrs. Abel? Mr. Price was here this afternoon?"

She thought she had told him. Yes, from about four until a little after six.

"I went by the Algonquin and picked him up at about four. Brought him here for—well, for what you could call a pep talk. To cheer him up and soothe him down. To try to convince him that he'd be wonderful in the part. And that he'd been in the business long enough not to have stage fright. Not that they ever get over it—not the good ones, anyway. Every time they go on it's a challenge, an excitement. I can remember when I—" She stopped abruptly. "No," she said, "I guess I can't. I gave Ken a few sips of champagne and then a couple of poached eggs on toast. And a lot of sisterly advice. Well, advice anyway. A pep talk, as I said."

Shapiro said that from what he had seen on the stage of the Rolf Simon Theater, the talk had worked. "Did Mr. Price happen to make a telephone call while he was here? About five o'clock, say?"

"He couldn't have if he'd wanted to, Lieutenant. The phone was out of order. Anyway, Clarice and I thought it was. Actually, we found out that she'd failed to set it right on its base—the kitchen extension phone, I mean. But we found that out after Ken had left. So, no. He certainly didn't call anyone from here this afternoon."

169

16

They were halfway down the corridor leading to the elevator when Kenneth Price appeared at the end of it, moving toward them. His expression was festive, as became a man on his way to a celebration for two. He walked with a springy step. The festive air vanished when he saw Shapiro and Cook. His walk slowed, and a few feet from them, he stopped.

"You two do get around, don't you?" Price said. "Been badgering Martha, I suppose. Checking up on me?"

"You could call it that," Shapiro said. "Checking up. I wouldn't call it badgering. I don't think Mrs. Abel will. Seems you were here this afternoon from about four o'clock on, and that you didn't make a telephone call at about five."

"I told you that."

"Yes."

"Most of the time I was listening to a pep talk," Price said. "All I got all day, seems like. Come on, boy. Pull up your socks. You can do it. Hell, you'd think I'd never played a part before, or that I was some kid going to his first prom or something. Damn it all, I'm a pro. I don't need all this bucking up. I've played tougher parts. And I was all right tonight. You two see the play? God knows you were at the theater afterward—quizzing me, for one thing."

Cook answered for both of them. He said, "We saw Act One

170

and part of Act Two. And I thought you were good, Mr. Price. Damn good."

"I was all right. The CBS reviewer came through. 'A skilled and subtle performance.' Said it gave a new dimension to the play. Whatever the hell he meant by that."

"Sounds good to me," Shapiro said. "You say you were getting pep talks all day? From more than Mrs. Abel?"

"It was all right from her," Price said. "Fine from her. After all, she's my—agent." Shapiro thought he had been about to use another word and had caught himself. "Girl," perhaps? Or "lover." It didn't matter.

"Encouragement from everybody, damn near," Price was saying. "Simon himself. Kirby. Hell, even our playwright. 'Come on, boy. You're not as lousy as you think you are.' Only, I didn't think I was—lousy, or going to be. Oh, I was keyed up. Maybe it showed. But all this goddamn back-patting. Jeez!"

"All this afternoon?"

"Martha this afternoon. The rest just before curtain, just before I was due to go on for that opening scene with Arlene. Everybody coming around to the dressing room at the last minute. To see if I was still alive, you'd have thought. See that I hadn't fainted or something."

"Mr. Simon? The director—Kirby? And Mr. Askew? All to buck you up?"

"All of them. And even the kid, Pete Withers. Even the kid, for God's sake."

"All wishing you well," Cook said, "even the playwright."

"Yes, even Askew. He was probably really the one who had the jitters. Jittery sort of guy, Askew is. Hell, if I had his money . . . but writers are funny birds, I guess."

"I'm not so sure Askew is really such a funny bird," Shapiro told Cook as they walked toward the Algonquin.

171

The buffet tables were set up in the hotel's lounge. The lobby was almost filled with men and women having their after-theater supper. And, of course, drinks to go with it. One of the men was Bret Askew. Celebrating? Tony and Nathan said, thank you, no, to a waiter captain who offered to seat them. They went to telephone booths. Both called Bellevue Hospital.

Edgar Lord had not made it, Tony was told. He had not regained consciousness or said anything before he died that a listening detective from the precinct squad could hear.

Shapiro talked to a doctor in the emergency ward, who said, sure, he knew of Donnatal Extentabs. A combination of belladonna-related alkaloids used by some internists in the treatment of peptic ulcer and for irritable bowel syndrome. Yes, substituted for the usual dosage of four tenths of a milligram of atropine sulfate. Advantage, one Extentab every twelve hours instead of one four-tenths-of-a-milligram atropine tablet four times a day. Well, yes, he supposed a couple of Extentabs could produce symptoms of atropine poisoning. Not severe poisoning—the belladonna alkaloids weren't all that drastic. Blurred vision, dilation of the pupils, yes. "Listen, Lieutenant, we're busy as hell here. And I'm a general surgeon. You want an internist. And maybe an eye man. O.K.?"

Shapiro said it was O.K., and thanks. He called precinct and arranged for a man from the precinct Homicide Squad to go to the Algonquin lounge for a drink, and to keep an eye on one Bret Askew, playwright. Not that Askew would be likely to go anyplace except up to his suite and to bed. Askew had no reason to believe that he needed to go anyplace.

Bret Askew wouldn't know until the next day how little cause he had to celebrate.

17

"It's not that I don't like it there, Tony," Rachel Farmer said. "You know I like it there. Only it's a little bit breaking my neck. Just a little, really."

It was almost twenty-four hours since Cook and Shapiro had visited Martha Abel in her penthouse, and since they had listened to Kenneth Price's complaints about unneeded encouragement. Rachel and Tony had both got to their Gay Street apartments at a little after ten, and both had already had dinner, if you could call it that. And both had read the brief, front-page story in the last edition of the New York *Sentinel*. It was below the fold. (The National League East and the American League West races were heating up as they neared the finish, and they took the space above the fold.)

The headline on the short story read:

PLAYWRIGHT HELD
IN SLAYING

Rachel and Tony had had brief nightcaps and gone to bed. They chose her bed, which is wider. Her apartment is also one flight lower.

Now Tony said, "Sorry, baby." He removed his right arm from under her neck and his left hand from a breast. "It's too nice a neck to break."

173

She said, "Thank you, Tony. And I quite like the arm. And it's such a nice little play. So gay. I'm sorry. They've killed that word, haven't they? 'Gay,' I mean."

Tony agreed that "they" had pretty much done in the word "gay" and that it was a pity. And that he too had liked *Summer Solstice*. What he had seen of it.

"Was the old man—the dresser, I mean—trying to blackmail Mr. Askew, Tony?"

That was the way it looked; obviously the way it looked— looked after hours of questioning by Shapiro and a man from the D.A.'s office. "With me just sitting in. Saying, 'Yes, that's what he told us,' when that was needed, Rachel. Nate's echo, you could call it."

The man from the D.A.'s office had been Bernard Simmons, chief of the D.A.'s Homicide Bureau. And Askew's lawyer had been present.

"Very expensive lawyer. Pretty famous one. Wouldn't let Askew answer most of our questions. What he was there for, of course. Very high-powered man, Simmons says. Going to be very tough all the way through. Simmons isn't too happy about any of it. But he did O.K. the charge. And he will take it to the grand jury. And he does expect an indictment. After that, he says, God knows. After all, Askew is an Askew. Oodles of money. And what have we got? Motive. Opportunity. Neither of them exclusive, far's we can prove."

She raised her head from the pillow, and Tony put his arm under it. For a moment they lay quietly together. Then Rachel said, "Go on, dear. An indictment for Branson's murder?"

"No. They'll hold that in reserve, for use if needed. For Lord's. The fingerprint is tangible. Jurors like fingerprints, Simmons says."

"What fingerprint, Tony? You hadn't said anything about a fingerprint."

"On the tennis racket that was used to bash Lord's head in. Not on the grip. That's some sort of make-believe leather. On up the handle, near the head. Where it's nice smooth wood that takes prints. It's taken a lot, the lab boys say. Mostly Price's, as you'd expect. But a couple of nice clear ones of Askew's. 'And how did they get there, Mr. Askew?'"

Askew's lawyer, J. Burton Livingston, had let his client answer that. The answer was that Askew hadn't any idea. Yes, he remembered seeing the racket in Price's dressing room, near the door. It was a necessary prop for a second-act scene. And possibly, just possibly, he might have picked it up at some time. He didn't remember doing so, but apparently he had. If it really had his prints on it.

"I play a good deal of tennis," Askew had said. "Not much good at it, but it is my game. Say I'm an addicted tennis player. When I see a racket—well, chances are I pick it up. Just to get the feel of it, the heft, the balance. Could be I picked this one up, without really being aware I was doing it."

"And Nate thinks that's possible," Tony went on. "Nate's sort of a tennis nut himself. He says yes, he often picks up a racket he doesn't have any idea of playing with just to get the heft of it, the balance. More or less a reflex, he agrees. One a good many players probably have."

"It's a good explanation," Rachel said. She paused a moment, and added, "I think. It convinces me. Won't it convince the jury?"

"The jury's not likely to hear it," Tony said. "Livingston and his helpers aren't fools. They'll investigate it—and find out we already have. Been at it for hours, half a dozen of us. Talking to

175

Askew's relatives and friends. There are quite a lot of Askews around. Most of them have places in Westchester and on Long Island. Places with tennis courts. Bret Askew has visited all of them. And he never plays tennis. Never has, far's his relatives know. I dug up a cousin who has a place in Westchester. Name of Clifford Askew. Two courts on his place, and Bret was there for a good many weekends. And never played tennis. Thinks it's a childish game. Doesn't play golf, either. Not the athletic type. His game is chess. So—neck all right now, baby?"

Rachel's neck was fine. Not breaking anymore. "And was the racket really the weapon somebody—Askew, as you and the lieutenant think—used to kill Lord?"

They were sure enough. It had been pounded down on something, the lab said. Pounded hard on something hard, like a skull not quite protected by a derby hat. (Which Lord probably had thought of as a bowler.) There were traces of the hat fabric where the strings looped through one side of the steel frame, and, although that was not yet certain, probable traces of blood. There hadn't been time, apparently, to wipe the racket clean. Or it hadn't seemed worth the trouble, since the use of the steel-framed racket pointed at Price, which was where Askew wanted things to point.

"Probably the reason he used it in the first place. To tie it to Price. When—well, when he got scared. Probably because of what Lord had seen at the party, or told Askew he'd seen. Also, the racket was handy. Just waiting to be used after he'd enticed Lord to the theater to pick up Branson's makeup. He pretended to be Price on the phone. And he got behind the door of the dressing room when Price was out of it—he probably told Lord to come at a time when he knew the room would be empty. He knew the sequences. After all, he'd written the play. So Lord

176

went on into the dressing room, probably, to look for his 'package,' and Askew slugged him from behind. Slugged him hard enough to spring the racket frame and put enough tension on the strings to break one of them. According to the lab boys, that is."

They would never, now, know what Lord had seen at Branson's last party—his surprise party. Or what he had told Askew he'd seen. Whatever had made him dangerous enough to the playwright to need killing. Askew wasn't telling, and Lord couldn't tell. A hand holding a twist of paper over a glass, presumably. Askew's hand and Branson's glass. And, they could assume, Lord had agreed to Askew's insistence that he tell the police he'd gone up to bed at eleven. So that he couldn't have seen barbiturate dropped into a glass at around a quarter of twelve, when they assumed it was.

"You and Nathan have to assume quite a lot of things, don't you?" Rachel said. "I can understand why this Mr. Simmons is dubious."

"Nate does the assuming," Tony told her. "And he's very good at it. We'll dig around some more. Probably come up with more. Maybe from the caterer's men. Almost certainly somewhere, now we know where to look and what to look for."

"You say Askew had a motive," Rachel said, and turned a little toward Tony. "For the dresser, I can see. And to throw suspicion on Mr. Price. Yes, I can see that. Took this stuff that made his eyes bulge—sort of bulge, anyway—after he'd had drinks with Price, so that it would look as if Price were trying to poison him because he had something on Price. Yes, I can see why he'd do that. I guess I can, anyway."

"Sometimes," Tony said, "they can't leave well enough alone. And sometimes that helps us catch them. Murderers, I mean."

She said she knew what he meant, for heaven's sake, and if he

177

would only listen. Why had Askew wanted Branson dead? "The leading actor in Askew's own play. The man who was the play's biggest draw and—"

She stopped and left the sentence hanging.

"Yes," Tony said, "because he was so important to the play's success. But after the reviews, and probably in Askew's own opinion too, his importance had turned around. Maybe he was important to the failure of the play, not its success. Because he was fatally miscast."

"But just for a play, Tony? It wasn't as if Askew had to have a success because he needed the money. To kill a man, apparently a nice enough man, just to keep a little comedy running. It's not as if *Summer Solstice* were—well, *Hamlet*."

"No. But in a way—well, I suppose in a way Askew thought of it as if it were. A shining thing, almost a sacred thing. A thing more important than anything else. Seems absurd to us. But then we aren't writers and, as somebody said a while back, writers are funny people. Don't always get things in perspective, I guess."

She did not reply to that, but turned to him for a good-night kiss. It did not stop with that, as neither had supposed it would.